Tye Watkins

In

VENDETTA

Vendetta

Other Books in the Tye Watkins Series

Border Trouble

The Crossing

Yancey

Desperate Trail

Drums Along the Border

Back To the Rockies

Second Chance

Yahzie-Apache Warrior

U.S. Marshal

A Reason To Kill

El Diablo

Gary McMillan

Published by Authors' Discovery   May 2018

Cover concept by Michael McMillan

Printed in the United States of America

Contents

Gary McMillan

Tye Watkins

In

Laredo

Chapter One

"There he is over there by them there boulders," Johnson whispered to his partner Tex Longley while pointing toward the spot with the barrel of his Henry repeater. "Looks like he's taking a leak," he chuckled.

"It'll be his last," Tex whispered as he laid the barrel of his old fifty caliber Sharps on a boulder to steady his aim at the sheep man.

Jose Vasquez was a twenty year old sheep herder working for Salvador Sanchez owner of the Sanchez Ranch. He has worked here most of his life as have most of the men working for Senor Sanchez. The ranch was the largest sheep ranch in the State of Texas totaling more than one hundred thousand acres. The ranch was bounded on the west by the Rio Grande River and extended east for miles into the arid regions of south Texas.

He had an old worn out Colt single action pistol stuck in the sash he wore around his waist. He was not familiar with the use of it but Senor Sanchez had insisted all his men go armed because of the recent troubles. A herder by the name of Hector Mendoza had been killed two weeks ago so the men working for Sanchez were armed. No one had been arrested for the murder by Sheriff Raul Espinosa as of yet so all hands were a little on edge.

When Jose finished relieving himself he glanced at the hill about five hundred paces away and saw a puff of smoke. The next instant something hit him in the chest and knocked him backwards against a large boulder. The heavy fifty caliber slug exploded his chest and left a hole in his back as it exited as large as man's fist. Jose never heard the 'boom' of the Sharps. He lay on the boulder his arms and legs hanging down the side.

"Damn, Tex," Johnson said slapping his friend on the shoulder, "You done blowed that stinking Mex back ten feet or more." He stood up, "Lets me and you go take a look."

"He's just a dead Mexican," Tex said reloading the old single shot Sharps. "Let's get the hell away from here."

Both men worked for the Lazy B Ranch owned by Sam and Linda Mason. The Lazy B was a cattle ranch and was relative small compared to the Sanchez spread. The ranch covered about ten thousand acres and ran about fifty five hundred head of beef which Sam was coming to realize was too many for this country where grass and water were scarce. He needed more land and the best available was already owned by the Sanchez family.

James Johnson was a small man about five foot seven and weighing maybe one hundred and forty pounds after a good meal. He was thirty years old and had left Arizona a few months earlier after killing a man in a saloon over the favors of one of the girls working there. He was thought to have been involved in several more but nothing was ever proven but his welcome in Arizona had played out. Truth is he was more than just a fair hand with the Colt strapped on his hip and had killed around fourteen men, some in a fair fight and some in the back for money.

Johnny "Tex" Longley was a cold blooded killer. Besides being an excellent shot with the long gun he was as was commonly called 'hell on wheels' with the forty-four caliber Colt in the tied down holster low on his hip. Known for his fiery temper he was a man not to be messed with.

Besides his gun handling ability he was known for his ability to fight with his fist and had killed one man with them. He was big of statue, six foot four and well over two hundred pounds and all muscle. Add all together, his size, his use of guns and fist, his temper; he was a very dangerous man to tangle with.

The situation in Laredo was bad and getting worse every day. Not only did you have the individual outlaws passing through but you have outlaw gangs doing the same and while in town lots of bad things were happening. On top of these problems you had another breed, the gunman or shootist who were generally loners. This breed, the shootist, were proud of their reputation as 'being quick on the draw' but for the most part were in shootouts with men of lesser ability. Two men with equal reputations were leery of confronting each other knowing both were probably take a little lead. For the gunman they generally stayed on the supposedly right side of the law with most shootings deemed justified.

Then you had gunman like "Tex" Longley whose gun was for hire. These men had no morals and no qualms about killing another man either in a supposedly fair fight or shooting them in the back. He was known to have killed twelve men in these supposedly fair fights but no one knew how many others like the recent young sheep herder he had killed.

The next morning Salvador Sanchez stormed into Sheriff Raul Espinosa's office. He had the blanket wrapped body of twenty year old Jose Vasquez tied on the back of a horse outside the jail.

"This is the second one of my men killed lately sheriff," he shouted his face twisted in anger. "What have you done about the first one-NOTHING," he shouted his voice becoming even louder. "I know who is doing this and you know, yet you do nothing."

"Calm down my friend," Raul said in a voice that did not betray his anger at the rancher who had stormed into his office. "Just calm down. Here my friend," he said handing the man a tin cup. "Let me fill your cup with coffee and we can talk."

Deputy's Tye Watkins and San Jenkins had left Fort Clark early the day before and traveled all day and most of the night stopping only to rest their mounts and drink some coffee. Both were tuckered out and in bad moods. In fact, since receiving the wire from their boss directing them to Laredo to see what was going on their moods had darkened. Neither had been involved in anything like stopping a range war that was brewing. A merchant in Laredo, Bill Fletcher, had contacted the U.S. Marshals' office in San Antonio that there was a problem there and the sheriff could not or would not find a solution. Both deputies wondered why the sheriff had not requested help instead of a merchant.

About noon they entered the outskirts of Eagle Pass where a little over a month ago Tye had killed the brutal murderer 'El Diablo'.

"Let's stable the horses and spend the night here," Tye said.

A grateful Sam nodded his head and mumbled, "Sounds good to me. I could use a damn bath also."

"Yeah, me too."

"I noticed," Sam said laughing.

"You're pretty damn ripe yourself," Tye chuckled. He looked around at the town he had left four or five weeks ago after the twister had devastated most of the town and was amazed at the new buildings that had gone up. He started to say he wanted to visit his friend Sheriff Hruska after bathing but was stopped before he could say anything.

"Tye Watkins," a voice boomed out from the bat-winged doors of a saloon on the left side of the street. "What in the blazes you doing back down here?"

Tye recognized the voice immediately as being Hruska's. "Passing through on our way to Laredo," he said dismounting and shaking his friends hand. "How's the shoulder?" Hruska had been wounded by Jeb Summers alias *El Diablo,* before Tye had tracked him down and after a vicious knife fight had killed the killer. Tye had received a serious cut on his left forearm and had almost bled to death before getting back to Eagle Pass and a doctor.

"Good as new," Hruska answered rotating his arm in a circular motion. "How about your arm?"

"Not at full strength yet but it will do." He turned to Sam who was still in the saddle. "Sam, this is one of the best if not the best damn sheriff in the whole State of Texas. Hruska took a couple of steps and reached and shook Sam's hand.

"J.A. Hruska," he said shaking the deputy's hand.

"Sam Jenkins," Sam said leaning down from the saddle and shaking the big man's hand. "Heard a lot about you for a long time but just never got down here to meet you.

Would have been here with Tye but that damn breed put a hole in me with his rifle."

"Seems like that bastard damn near killed each one of us before Tye sent him to hell," Hruska said. He looked at Tye. "Now back to you my friend, what brings you down here?"

"I was going to look you up after cleaning up a bit but let's just go to your office and palaver some about things going on in Laredo."

Hruska had a surprised look on his face. "Laredo! How did you hear about the trouble brewing down there?'

"A merchant named Fletcher had contacted our office in San Antonio and asked us to look into it."

"Bill and Marie Fletcher; they own the general store there and are good people, honest as the day is long. Bill had a store here for a long time before Timothy Jones came here with a lot of money, questionable I might add, and opened a huge store and lower prices. So Espinosa didn't contact ya'll?"

"Not that we know of," Sam answered. "Who is this Espinosa?"

"Lets go to my office and have a cup of coffee and maybe I can fill you in a little on what's happening down there." Sam dismounted and led both horses and followed the two men to the Sheriff's office where Hruska poured a cup of coffee for each of them and all sat down around the desk. Sam noticed what Tye had noticed a few weeks before when he first came in the office; it was immaculate.

Hruska took a sip, winched as the tin cup burned his lips as it always does and then set the cup on the desk and folded his hands in front of him on the desk. "What you have in Laredo is a mess but probably not that complicated to figure out. Raul Espinosa is the sheriff and he along with two deputies Frank and Jesus, don't know their last names, pretty well run the town with an iron fists. I've heard they have their fingers in just about every business there. You know what I mean; you pay protection fee or else bad things could happen." He took another sip of coffee.

"We've seen the type before," Sam said.

Hruska opened a drawer and pulled out a sheet of paper. "I've started a letter to your boss about the situation there but have not finished it yet because I'm still checking out a few things and don't want to mess things up with information that's not true. Since you are here I guess I can throw it away and just tell you what I know." He stood up and walked over and picked up the coffee pot and refilled each coffee cup. Sitting back down he took a bottle of whiskey out of the drawer and put a little in each cup. "Makes it a little sweeter," he chuckled.

"Salvador Sanchez and his wife Marie own the largest sheep ranch in Texas. It is south and southeast of Laredo and covers around a hundred thousand acres on which he runs sixty to seventy thousand sheep. He is an honorable man. The ranch has been in his family as long as anyone can remember, at least a hundred years or more. There are several much smaller ranches around, some cattle and other small sheep ranches."

"Everything was fine till a couple or three months ago when one of his hands was shot and killed while watching a flock of sheep. Another was goaded into fist fight and was damn near beat to death. Since then Senor Sanchez has all his men armed even though three fourths don't have a clue how to handle sidearm or a rifle."

"That's not a good situation," Tye said. "If they are shot and killed and have a gun in their hand it could be called self defense by whoever shot them. Any clues who could be causing the trouble?"

"Couple years ago an outfit came to Laredo and bought ten thousand acres of land north of Laredo. The owner is a man named Samuel Mason and he runs about five thousand or so head of cattle which are too many for the ranch."

"Five thousand head on ten thousand acres doesn't seem too many," Sam said.

Hruska nodded and smiled. "Most places it would be fine but out here the grass is not so plentiful as other places. Five thousand could survive but would be a little thin, not prime beef. He needs more land or less cattle if he's gonna make a success of his ranch."

"What do you know about the men working for both ranches," Tye asked.

Hruska scratched his chin for a few seconds before answering. "Don't know very many of the hands but almost all of Sanchez's men have been with him for years. Some are young but they have been raised on the ranch as their pa's worked there. The only man I know at Mason's ranch is the foreman, Bill Gleason. He's one of the best cowmen around and is honest a man as I've ever been around. I don't think he would be working for anyone who is a little on the shady side. I've heard the owner, Mason, has two gun slicks working for him that don't know a steer from a bull but that don't make them bad guys."

"No it don't," Tye said, but it makes a man wonder why a rancher would hire hands that don't know anything about cattle."

"Sam and me are going to get a room and wash some of this trail dust off. Let's meet a little later for some supper and talk some more." They shook hands and agreed to meet at the restaurant across from the sheriff's office at eight.

As Sam and Tye walked out Hruska hollered. "Forgot to mention that there are a couple gun slicks in town. No papers on them but I'm watching them pretty close."

"Any names," Sam asked?

"Billy Williams and James Dyson but goes by Red."

"Damn," Sam said then added, "Double damn."

"You know one of them or both of them," Tye asked.

"Don't know Billy but I've had my run in with Red. I got the drop on him about three years ago when he came out of store after robbing three people that were in the store as well as the cash register in the store. Since he had no prior record the judge only gave him two years of hard labor. He whispered to me as he was led out of the court room we would meet again someday."

"He good with a gun?"

"I've heard he's damn good. He's killed four or five men but all face to face in fair fights so there's no papers on him. I figure the character named Billy is just like him as far as handling a gun. I guess the day of reckoning is here for me and him."

Chapter Two

Back in Laredo Senor Sanchez and Sheriff Espinoza have been having a heated discussion in the sheriffs' office on the situation with Sanchez men being killed.

"I want something done Raul and quickly. If one more of my men are killed I swear to you there will be war. You know, I know, everyone knows who is doing the killing- the gunman who calls himself Tex who works for Mason."

"Si Senor Sanchez but one has to prove it. There has not been one witness who has come forward that can say they saw anything."

"What about the gun, the fifty caliber Sharps that is being used."

Espinosa nodded his head. "That is a clue Senor but I can tell you the names of a dozen men who have one and they are probably more I don't know about. I am working on the problem Senor."

Sanchez stood up quickly knocking his chair over. "As I said, not one more of my men had better die." He turned and stormed out of the office.

Espinosa smiled. The next step in his bosses plan would blow the lid off and the war between cattleman and sheep men would be full blown. He and his men would make sure that neither Sanchez nor Mason would survive nor any of their family.

After a bath and putting on clean clothes Sam and Tye strolled over to the restaurant to get some vittles. Walking through the door they immediately spotted Hruska who was motioning for them to come on over. As soon as they sat down at the table with the sheriff he was telling them the news.

"Red, or James Dyson, knows you are in town and is talking about what a piece of horse shit you are Sam. Saying the town needs to be rid of you and he's going to do it."

"Where's he at," Sam asked?

"My deputy is watching both of them over at the Ace High saloon."

"No sense in making the man wait." Sam said scooting his chair back and standing up. He slipped his Colt out and spun the chamber making sure it was loaded and dropped it back in the holster then lifted it a little to make sure it would come out easy.

"Guess those vittles will have to wait awhile," Tye said standing up and doing the same as Sam with his Colt. "You coming sheriff?"

"Hell yes! Wouldn't miss this for the world. Besides, Sam will need a witness besides his partner."

The three lawmen walked through the bat-winged door of the salon and immediately spotted the men they were looking for. They were holding court with the patrons telling them what a piece of shit Sam was.

The circle of men parted and all backed away from the two men when they saw the lawmen come in.

Sam spoke first. "I hear you are looking for me Red. I'm here so whatever you need to do, do it."

"Be kind of hard lawman when you have the cavalry with you," Red replied looking at Tye and Hruska

"This is between you and me Red. As long as your partner there keeps that gun of his in his holster these men will stay out of it. I took you down once after you robbed that store and I can do it again. Guess two years in the prison didn't straighten you out."

Red laughed. "All you law dogs and judges think that prison is a place to send a man to rehabilitate him. Hell, with the poor food, beatings, and everything else that goes on there it only makes a man more bitter than ever. For two years I was starved and beat for no damn reason other than the guards enjoyed doing it and all I could think of was getting you for putting me here. That idea kept me alive. The only thing that scared me was someone might just up and kill you before I had a chance to."

"I'm here now Red so either fill your hand or drop the gun belt," Sam said.

Red's partner stepped two steps to the left and made it obvious to everyone he had no intention of staying out of the fracas. A tense few seconds passed and then Sam saw Red's eyes squint just a little and an instant later Red's hand dropped to the butt of his Colt as did his partners.

It was something the men in the saloon would never forget. No one seen the guns materialize in the two marshals hands until two blasts from their Colts sounded as one and the two outlaws were blasted into eternity with neither barely getting their guns up and out of their holsters. Hruska looked in amazement. He had drawn his but it was over before he could pull the trigger. There was dead silence in the room as the smoke from the Colts slowly rose in the air to the ceiling.

One bystander finally managed to move over to the two bodies on the floor. He looked down at both and whistled. "Both men are hit about the second button on their shirts."

Other men walked over and stared at the two men. One man turned toward Sam and Tye who were reloading their Colts. "Been all over this here country and seen more than one gunfight. Saw Hickok once and Doc Holliday shoot a man two different times. Both of them were fast but hell man, I never even saw either of your hands move. All I can say is 'Gawd a mighty'." There were a few chuckles among the other men but they felt the same way; they just were witnesses to probably the two fastest men around and it was something they would never forget and unfortunately would tell everyone they met about it. That is how reputations were born and resulted in other men who thought they were the fastest and wanting to prove it.

Sheriff Hruska spoke up pointing to a big fellow with a blue shirt. "Harry, you go get the doctor." Doc Lambert served as doctor, vet, and mortician and walked in the door just as Harry was walking out.

The doc looked at Hruska. "Hear the shooting and figured I'd be needed as he hurried over to the two men lying on the floor.

"Don't need no doctoring Doc" one of the men standing by the bodies said as Lambert rushed over. Them thar two were deader than a dang piece of driftwood fore they hit the floor."

Doc felt for pulses then stood up and looked at Hruska then noticed Tye standing beside him. "Well I be horns waggled, Tye Watkins."

"Good to see you again, Doc." Several heads looked at the man Doc just called Tye Watkins. Tye shook Docs hand and introduced him the Sam. "Sam this old codger is Doc lambert." As the two men shook hands Tye added. "This is the man who sewed me up after the Breed cut me pretty bad."

"Glad to meet you Doc and thanks for saving Tye's sorry hide. Course no one cared except for his wife and kids," he chuckled. Everyone laughed.

"A man of fifty or so walked over to them and looked at Tye. "You the scout at Fort Clark?"

"Yes, sir, I was for years but now I'm a Deputy U.S. Marshal and chasing down outlaws instead of Apaches."

The man stuck out his hand which Tye took. "Always hoped to meet you some day but never figured I would. My son is in the cavalry at Fort Clark. He's a sergeant and has told me a lot of stories in his letters about you. One in particular where you stood over him fighting off Apaches when he was injured in a battle at the Rio Pecos and Rio Grande River junction. In another letter he said all was lost when they were overrun by Apaches when you picked up a rifle by the barrel and screaming something fierce charged down the gulley swinging the rifle and bashing heads. Said the Apache were so startled by this crazy white man they retreated and rode off."

Tye laughed. "That was a long time ago sir. Is your son Sergeant Larry Barstow?"

"Yes it is. I'm George Barstow."

"I can tell you this Mr. Barstow; you have every right to be proud of your son. He is as fine a soldier as I have ever known and by the way, he's a fine gentleman. You should be very proud of him."

"Thanks for those words Tye. Me and the missus worry about him every day and I'm proud to know he is the man I wanted him to be."

"He is Mr. Barstow, and he has the respect of every man on the post including Major Thurston. It was nice meeting you sir and when I get back to Clark I will tell Sergeant Barstow I met you and you wish him well." He shook the fathers hand and then turned to Sheriff Hruska. "Wasn't we fixing to get some vittles before all this started?"

Chapter Three

It took Tye and Sam three and half days to cover the distance from Eagle Pass to Laredo. They didn't learn much more at supper the night before they left. Both knew they were riding into a mess, one they had not dealt with before and could prove very explosive with a lot of dead people left in its wake. It needed to be dealt with quickly.

As they neared the town of Laredo they put their marshal's badges away figuring it might be easier to get a handle on things if people didn't know they were lawmen. Both men wore vest so they put the badges in their shirt pockets with the leather vest covering them.

"What's the plan?"

Tye thought for a moment. "Let's visit the merchant that asked for help, Mr. Fletcher. Hruska vouched for him so I figure he can be trusted to keep quiet. It didn't take long to find a building that had a sign reading General Store and had Bill Fletcher owner written on it. They reined their mounts in front and dismounting wrapped their reins around the hitching rail. They took off their hats and beat the trail dust from them on their legs and placing them back on walked into the coolness of the store where a bell rang when the door opened. The lawmen looked at a store that first of all was clean and neat and looking like they had about everything a family or ranch hand would want. Rifles, sidearm's, ammunition, shovels rakes, nails, saddles and blankets, canned food, furniture, and all kinds and colors of cloth plus a hundred other items. It was impressive.

A man came through a door that Tye figured led to the man's living quarters. He looked to be in his forties and appeared to be fit and in good shape unlike most store owners. He wore dark pants and white shirt with a black bowstring tie and Tye could tell it wasn't fat under the shirt.

"Can I help you gentlemen?"

"You Mr. Fletcher," Tye asked?

The man nodded. "What can I help you with?"

"Just some information if we can go somewhere we can talk," Tye said taking out his badge and showing it to the man.

"Thank God you have come," he said shaking their hands not asking for names. Follow me and he walked back through the door he had come out of. As Tye figured his home was like the store, clean and neat.

"My name is Tye Watkins and this hombre is Sam Jenkins. We are United States Deputy Marshals and are here in answer to your letter to the office in San Antonio.

"You the famous scout at Fort Clark?"

Sam winced as usual when this question was invariably asked when anyone heard the name.   *Is there a damn person in the whole State that has not heard of Tye? Likely not,* he mused smiling.

"First things first Mr. Fletcher. We need for you to be quiet about us being here so maybe people will talk and let things slip that they not say otherwise if they knew we were lawmen. To answer your question I was a scout at Fort Clark till about three years ago when I became a marshal."

"I can't believe you are in my home. I've been hearing stories about you for years and now, here you are."

Next came the line that Sam had heard a hundred times. Tye said, "Don't believe everything you hear. Stories get exaggerated."

"Your secret is safe with me." He motioned to a couple chairs. "Please sit and we can talk. I'm glad you came so quickly. Another of Sanchez's men was shot a killed three days or so ago. It is my understanding that Senor Sanchez told the sheriff that if one more man is killed it was war with the cattle rancher Sam Mason."

"Why is he pointing to Mason as the trouble maker," Sam asked?

"The men killed were shot with an old fifty caliber Sharps, you know one of those old buffalo guns. One of the men working for Mason, a Tex Longley has one. It is known Mason needs more land for the number of cattle he has."

"What do you know about this Mason fellow," Tye questioned?

"He and his wife cane here about two years ago and bought land north of here, about ten thousand acres along the Rio Grande. I personally think they are fine people and are not involved in any of this. Bill Gleason is their foreman and I know him from when I was in Eagle Pass. There's not a man I know of that knows more about cattle than him and as far as I know he is as honest as the day is long. There are four ranch hands and all seem to be honest, ride for the brand type of cow hand. There are two others I don't know very well but both are of questionable character and from what I can see couldn't tell a steer from a heifer. Both wear their guns low and tied down. I already told you about one of them, Longley who has a Sharps."

"What about the Sanchez's," Sam asked?

"Not a better family in Texas. The ranch has been in the family for a hundred years or so. They pay their bills and take care of the men and their families that work for them. They have around a hundred thousand acres of land and from what I hear, the largest sheep ranch in the State. I just can't figure out who or why is causing them the trouble. I know Mason needs either more land or fewer cattle but his land is not connected to the Sanchez's so why would he be causing trouble?"

"Yeah, why would he," Tye mumbled? Tye stood up and Sam followed. "We've been on the trail for a little over three days. My pard and me need to get us a room and clean up some. We'll talk more maybe tomorrow but let us nosey around some first. Remember, don't tell anyone about us till we're ready."

"Don't you worry none about that. See you tomorrow."

"Who was that you were talking to dear," Marie Fletcher asked?

"Just two out of work cowmen looking for work. Thought maybe I might know of a ranch looking for some hands. Told them to go the see Sam Mason."

"Well, supper is ready so come on into the kitchen."

Before starting to eat his meal and waiting on his wife to sit he spoke to his wife. "Marie, we have been married what, forty years and in all that time I have never lied to you. I can't start now."

"You going to tell me those men were not cow hands looking for work but are U.S. Deputy Marshals. Is that what you were going to say?" "Why did you let go on about them being cow hands?"

Bill shrugged his shoulders

"I knew it would not be long before you told me the truth. Didn't take very long did it," she quipped laughing.

Bill cleared his throat and grinned. "You know me like a book don't you. I guess you also heard they asked me to keep quiet about them being lawmen for awhile?"

She nodded. "I won't say a word but it's going to be difficult to keep quiet about Tye Watkins being in my house."

After obtaining a room and a bath the two lawmen walked to a restaurant the man at the hotel told them about. Sitting in a corner booth drinking coffee and waiting on their meal they studied the other patrons. It was a little early and there was only four other tables where people sat. One table was an elderly man and his wife which they ignored. Another table had a man in his thirties and a pretty little filly which appeared to be his wife or lady friend. They were talking law, holding hands and generally ignoring everyone else. Another table was more interesting; two Mexicans all wearing badges and were close enough for some of their conversation to be heard by Tye and Sam. The last table was a man, wife and two small children about seven to ten years old. The only interesting table was the table with the men with badges.

The lawmen could only pick up bits and pieces of the conversation and wished they were closer. The conversation was definitely about the trouble brewing. They picked up a couple names, one they already knew; Sam Mason and someone named J.T. Brimley. From the conversation it appeared something was fixing to happen. One of the men looked around and said something to the other two and they began talking in a much lower tone of voice, one that kept their voices from carrying to Tye's table. The lawmen filed the name of J.T. Brimley in their memory and would find out tomorrow who he was.

"Right now their plates were place in front of them by the pretty little waitress: thick steak, potatoes, and hot biscuits which they both dove into and forgot about talking or anything else for a few minutes. They ate their fill but did have a little room left for some of the best apple pie they had ever eaten.

"I tell you Tye," Sam said leaning back in his chair rubbing his belly and smiling. "After that meal I hope this case takes awhile to figure out.

"I don't," Tye replied. "Cause if it does Rebecca is going to have a lot of work when I get back letting out the pants and shirts." Both men laughed.

"Let's mosey over to the saloon across the street and see if we can pick up some loose talk there on what's going on," Tye suggested. They paid their two bits apiece for the meal and a tip and walked out of the restaurant and walked across the street to the saloon.

Looking through the bat-winged doors of the saloon they saw the same thing they had saw all over the state. The saloon was narrow maybe twenty feet wide with scattered tables mostly which because they figured it was early were empty. It was maybe forty feet long and had a bar, if you could call it that and it ran down one wall for maybe half the distance to the back. The bar was wooden planks sitting on empty kegs. The only thing different was there was not a picture of a nude lady on the wall above the bar. Everything else, smoke, dirty spittoons, the smell of unwashed bodies, and sawdust on the wooden floors were the same.

"Don't reckon I know you gents," the man behind the bar said as they walked up. The barkeep was a big man with rosy cheeks and a bulbous nose that indicated he partook of the merchandise fairly frequently. He wore what used to be white apron around his waist and had a Colt strapped on his hips which both lawmen knew was a little strange. The two got their bottle and moseyed over to a table close to two others that were occupied but not so close to be obvious.

The patrons all gave them the once over and a couple commented something they could not hear. Sam figured it was because of Tye's size more than anything else plus they were strangers in town with tied down guns on the hips.

They were on their third drink when the bat-winged door opened and two Mexicans walked in and sat down at a table next to theirs. Both men spoke to Tye and Sam and in a friendly way inquired if they were passing through or looking for work.

Tye answered them. "Can't say for sure. Guess we would stay if the right job came along."

"Evening boys," the barkeep said as he brought a bottle and two glasses. "Been on the range today, Johnny."

"Si Senor. Been gathering up all the lambs along with their mothers trying to get a count and looking for any diseases."

The barkeep nodded and said before he walked back to bar, "You take care Johnny and you to Joe." Johnny Rivera and Joe Gonzales worked for Senor Sanchez and had their whole adult lives.

Joe replied. "We try to be nice and quiet tonight, Senor Henry."

It was obvious to Tye and Sam these two were regular patrons of the saloon and the barkeep seemed to know them well. Both men had worn out forty-four caliber pistols. Neither had a holster and the guns were stuck down in a sash around their waist. The guns were probably fifteen or so years old and looked like they had not been cleaned in forever. Tye figured they would not even fire and if they did might just blow up.

Two more Mexicans walked in and these men were different. Both had Colts tied down on their hips and looked like they were well cared for. Also, both wore deputy badges. When the barkeep came over with a bottle his attitude was entirely different; no how ya'll doing tonight or not even and howdy-do. He set the bottle down and two glasses and walked off.

The bat-winged doors opened again several men came in. Three went to a table and two walked to the bar. Both Tye and Sam saw the two Mexicans in the table next to them watching the two men at the bar and spoke to each in hushed voices that barely reached Tye and Sam and not loud enough for the two men at the bar to hear.

"We had better leave," Johnny whispered to Joe. Joe nodded and both men laid some coins on the table and scooted their chairs back to get up.

At that instant one of the men turned and started sniffing the air. "Damn, Tex, I do believe I smell sheep shit in here."

Johnny making a big show of sniffing the air said, "You're right James and I think it's coming from right over there," nodding toward the two Mexicans getting up out of their chairs.

"We are leaving Senor Longley. We want no trouble," Johnny Rivera said walking toward the door.

Both of the men stepped between the two Mexicans and the door. "Not just yet Mex. We'll tell you when you can leave," Tex said and shoved the much smaller Mexican backwards into the other one and both men stumbled almost falling to the floor. The man called Tex was big, six foot four or so and well over two hundred pounds and packing no fat. The other was much shorter and maybe one hundred fifty soaking wet but he had the look of a dangerous man. Either man could handle the two sheep men by themselves and a blind man could see the two Mexicans were in trouble.

Tye glanced at the table with the two deputies sat. They were paying no attention to what was going unlike everyone else was. This surprised Tye and he nudged Sam who looked at the deputies.

"The smaller of the two Mexicans, the one called Johnny said. "Please Senor. No trouble tonight."

"Little late for that," he said and hit the man with a hard right fist the rocked the little mans to his heels. He landed on his back and to Tye's surprise started to get up and Tye could see fire in the eyes. Tye knew this was fixing to get real nasty and someone was going to die, maybe two.

Tye stood up and said. "Hey big boy, why don't you try picking on someone your own size."

Tex and James turned toward Tye. Tex said. "Just who the hell are you?"

"Just an old boy that don't like men who bully much smaller men and especially don't like a man who can't put a hobble on his lips."

That remark changed everything liked Tye figured it would. The two Mexicans were forgotten by the two men and all their attention were on Tye and then Sam when he stood up.

"Do you think these two hombres need a lesson in manners," Sam asked?

"Appears so since the two deputies have no interest in shutting up their mouths."

"Don't know who you men are but you are talking to Tex Longley."

"Tye laughed. "That name suppose to mean something Sam. You ever heard of a man by the name of Tex?"

"Nope! Can't say that I have."

"Don't shoot them Sam if you don't have to," Tye said in a low tone but loud enough for the two men to hear. Both men went for their guns but both stopped when they were half way out of their holsters. Both men looked at the wrong end of two forty-four caliber Colts aimed at their bellies.

"I figured you men were gun men but guess I was wrong. Neither one of you could beat my mother, rest her soul."

The two men were stunned as was everyone else including the two deputies as how quickly the Colts had materialized in their hands. Both men realized they should be dead.

"Drop your belts, men and do it really careful like and kick them over here." Both men did as they were told.

"Now you," Tye said nodded toward the big one called Tex, "Come over here." When Tex was in front of him Tye undid his gun belt and handed it to Sam. "Watch the other piece of horseshit while I teach this man some manners."

"You gonna fight me," a startled Tex mumbled a smile on his lips.

"Looks someone needs to teach you some manners. Obliviously your mom didn't, if you had one."

"Why you..." Tex screamed and cut loose with a right that he expected to end this fight real quick. Only problem was he hit nothing but air as Tye ducked the blow and countered with a tremendous right just above the belt buckle on the big man. Tex's eyes bulged and his mouth was open trying to suck in some air but all he got was a left that caught him full in the mouth and rocked him back on his heels.

Tye had to give the man credit. Tex roared like a bear and charged Tye trying to get him in a bear hug. Tye sidestepped stuck out his leg and tripped the man whose face hit the sawdust covered floor. He got up and was even madder now because the other patrons were laughing at his expense which never happened before. He had never been in the place of the men he had dominated and this sumbitch was whupping his butt and he hadn't even landed a blow.

Tex stood up swaying just a little but a hell of lot more leery of this bastard. He circled the man who just stood in one spot his hands hanging loosely at his sides and just turned his body to follow him as he circled. He suddenly swung a roundhouse right that missed as Tye stepped back a half step. He followed with a left that was blocked when Tye's right arm shot up and then a left from Tye caught him on the nose. The breaking of bone and cartilage caused some of the men to cringe. Another right caught Tex on the point of the chin lifting him off the floor and it was all over as his unconscious body crumpled to the wooden floor.

"Get your friend up off the floor and help him to his horse and go back to wherever you came from."

"What about our guns," James asked.

"They will be in the sheriff's office tomorrow. You and your friend can pick them up whenever," Tye said. "One other thing. I hoped you learned a lesson tonight that you don't go around bullying people because you just don't always know who you are messing with. By all rights, Sam and me could have shot you tonight and all these good people would say it was self defense.. Remember that. Now get the hell out of here." James helped Tex to his feet and the look Tex gave Tye sent a shiver up Sam's back.

After the two men left Tye walked over to the table with the two Mexican deputies sat. He looked down at the two who were staring in their drinks. Tye swept his hand across the table and knocked both beers from their hands.

"What kind of deputies are you anyway" he shouted? Neither looked up so Tye reached down to the nearest one and grabbing his collar jerked the man to his feet. "You were just going to sit there and let those two pieces of horseshit beat the hell out of this man or worse?" It wasn't really a question but a demand for an answer.

"I asked you a damn question," and looked down at the man's star and said as he ripped the star from the man's shirt. "You are a damn disgrace to that badge you piece of horse dung." He shoved the man hard into the table behind him knocking the table over with a crash and the Mexican sprawled on the floor on his back, his eyes as wide as saucers.

"And you ain't no better," he said jerking the second man to his feet and ripping off his badge and shoving him backwards to where he fell on top of his friend. "Both of you so-called lawmen get the hell out of my sight now or you both will be in your own damn jail.

Now git and be damn quick before I really get mad." Both scrambled to their feet and hurried out the door with raucous laughter from the other patrons ringing in their ears.

A man walked over to the table where Sam and Tye were sitting. He was a big man but mostly fat as far as Tye could tell. He was fifty or so and from the looks of his hands hadn't down any hard labor in a long time.

"Mind if I sit down for a moment" he asked.

"Suit yourself," Tye answered sharply his mad still racing through his veins. The man turned a chair around and sat down. Tye looked the man over. He was a little over fifty or so liked he figured at first glance, but something about him told him this was a dangerous man. He had steel grey eyes, dark brown hair that was showing a little gray around the temples. He was a little heavy but Tye's first impression was that he was fat didn't pan out now that he studied him a little closer. He was heavy but Tye and Sam both could see there was a hell of lot of muscle under the outer layer of fat and he had moved easily as he had walked toward them.

The man set the mug of beer down that he carried with him and looked at Tye for a few seconds before speaking. "My name is Bart Williams and I own a small ranch near Eagle Pass, the Lazy W. Just was wondering what you were doing down here in Laredo."

Tye looked at the man. "Do I know you friend?"

The man laughed. "No but God knows I know who you are Tye. I saw you awhile back in Eagle Pass when you were after that bastard, Jeb Summers or El Diablo as he called himself." The man spoke in a low tone. "Since you don't have a badge on I figured people didn't know who you were and for some reason you didn't want them to know."

Tye nodded and asked. "What are you doing here in Laredo Mr. Williams?"

I was a Ranger for a long time and then sheriff in Austin for awhile and then in Eagle Pass till some damn men came in one Saturday night and shot up the place and killed several town folks including my wife and young son. I killed those men, shot them down like the vermin they were without a trial by jury or given any due process of law they were entitled to. I resigned after that and had a little money saved up that I put down on some land southwest of Eagle Pass and got into ranching."

Sam spoke up and reached across the table and shook the man's hand. "I heard tell of that Mr. Williams. Heard that you were a damn good lawman too. Sorry about your family but me and some of the other deputies thought you were justified in doing what you did and only saved the county and state some money by not having to conduct a trial and plus house and feed those sumbitches till they were executed."

The man named Bart smiled and nodded. "I appreciate that. To answer your question Tye, I came here at the request of Bill Fletcher, an old friend of mine when he lived in Eagle Pass."

Tye nodded. I know Mr. Fletcher. He is the reason we are here. He wrote a letter to the U.S. Marshals office requesting help, but why are you here.?"

"Bill had asked me to come down and look around inconspicuous like and see if I could figure out what or who was behind all the trouble here. I guess he thought maybe the letter he told me about had gotten loss or something but he was afraid something bad was fixing to happen to some very good friends of his, the Sanchez's who have about the largest damn sheep ranch in the whole State of Texas."

"We've met Bill and asked him to keep our identity to himself and let us mix with the people and maybe learn something that we would not have if people knew were lawmen," Sam said.

"So I guess I'm to hobble my lip too."

Tye and Sam both grinned and nodded. Tye asked. "Have you learned anything nosing around since you have been here?"

"Not really. Got some ideas though."

"Well that's more than we have right now so let's hear your hunches," Tye said.

Bart took a swallow of his beer and wiped his lips with the sleeve of his shirt before saying anything. "Understand now that this here is just hunches, no basis for truth in them at all." He scratched the stubble on his chin. "I think the sheriff is either up to his eyeballs in this mess or he is covering for someone and getting paid to be quiet. I think he is as crooked as a snake."

Tye chuckled. "If those two deputies are any indication of the law around here I would tend to agree with your assessment."

"What about the two men we had the little run end with?" Sam asked.

"They work for the Masons out at the Lazy B. They are young and full of piss and vinegar but I think its all blow. Could be wrong though. Hadn't thought they might be involved till tonight."

"Why tonight," Tye asked?

"Those two deputies letting them get away with what they were doing to that Mexican youngster that works for Sanchez. Sorter odd don't you think?"

Tye nodded. "It is at that. You friends with Sheriff Hruska back in Eagle Pass?"

Bart laughed. "That is one tough sumbitch as you know, Tye. Tough he is, but fair and honest as the day is long. But yeah, to answer your question. We've been friends since he took over as sheriff after I quit.

Tye nodded. "It's been a long day. Let's turn in and get some shuteye and maybe think on things some and meet over at the restaurant for breakfast." The three men stood up and shook hands and headed to the hotel.

Tye lay awake for awhile mulling over the things going on around this town. All his cases before were pretty much cut and dried; had a name of a man that was wanted and he just tracked him down. This was different. There had been two murders and no sure fire suspects other than hunches and no apparent motives that he or Sam could come up with. "Yep, this was going to be real interesting," he mumbled to himself and rolled over and went to sleep.

Chapter Four

"Who's the man over there in the coat and tie eating by himself, "Tye asked Bart over a cup of coffee?

"That's the banker Mr. J.T. Brimley. Sorter the uppity type. You know, thinks himself a little better than you or me. Seems to run the bank okay. Fletcher likes him and he should know since Brimley is his banker and handles all his money," then added with a chuckle. "Not that Bill has that much."

At that time the door opened and a large Mexican with a badge came in, looked around and then headed for their table.

"Here comes trouble," Bart said quietly.

Tye studied the man as he walked across the room toward them. He also slipped the leather thong of the hammer of his Colt that held the gun in place. The man was large alright but mostly around his middle. He had a long mustache with the ends hanging below his chin and small black eyes under heavy black eyebrows. He had a scar on his left cheek that made him look like a bad hombre. Overall, Tye thought he was one ugly human being.

He stood at the edge of the table with his right hand hanging close to the pistol on his hip.

"Something you want sheriff?' Tye asked.

Sheriff Raul Espinoza recognized Tye from the description his deputies had given him. "I want to know why you treated my men the way you did last night?"

"Sure Sheriff. Sit down and have a cup of coffee and we'll talk about it."

"I don't want no damn cup of coffee mister. You assaulted an officer of the law last night and I want to know why. You need to come with me now." The other patrons were now paying attention.

"Sure thing sheriff, just as soon as I have my breakfast. You wouldn't want to arrest a man before he had his vittles now would you. That just ain't civilized."

Espinoza, taken back a little by Tye's remark puffed out his chest and said. "Get your gringo ass up now and placed his hand on the butt of his Colt.

Bart, sitting to the left of Sam slowly moved his hand toward his pistol. Sam reached over and put his hand on the old sheriff's arm to stop him. Bart looked at him and Sam smiled and shook his head.

"Sure thing sheriff," Tye said standing up. "But I still don't think its right to arrest a man that has an empty stomach." With that said, his gun magically appeared in his hand before the sheriff or anyone else realized the hand had moved.

"Gawdalmighty! Someone at one of the tables said loudly. "Did ya'll see that?"

The fat sheriff stood there with his mouth open and like everyone else, could not believe the lightning speed of Tye's draw. Bart looked at Sam, Sam just winked and smiled.

Tye said. "Now sheriff, sit down and let me eat and we will talk about last night and maybe a couple of other things. The sheriff stood there not moving. Tye's facial expression changed and   he said in a low, threatening tone, "I said sit."

Something about the way Tye looked at him or maybe it was the tone of his voice, or maybe the gun appearing magically made the sheriff have second thoughts and he slowly sat down with both hands on the table.

Nothing was said for a moment as the three men sipped their coffee and the nervous waitress poured the sheriff a cup. "What's this all about?"

"It's about your two deputies watching a man get beat half to death last night and just sitting there watching. If Sam and me had not stepped in the kid would have been dead. I simply told them how I felt about men who supposedly are paid to uphold the law and that they were a disgrace to the badge."

"They did not tell me this, just which you pulled a gun on them and took their badges and beat them up."

"I did not beat them up," Tye said before forking a mouth full of eggs in his mouth and washing them down with coffee. I simply told them what I thought of them, took their badges and gently shoved them to the floor." Sam nearly choked on his eggs.

"But, Senor, they were officers of the law an…"

"They had badges on sure enough, but they sure as hell weren't officers of the law and if you support trash like that I may begin to wonder about you."

"But I…." he paused. "Who do you think you are coming into my town and doing this to my men and…"

"As an officer of the law, Sheriff, you are paid to uphold the law are you not?"

"Si Senor but…"

"Two men were beating the hell of a man, one of your citizens, and your so called deputies just watched. Is that upholding the law?"

"I do no…"

"Dammit, yes or no?""

Espinosa shook his head. "No Senor, but it does not change the fact you attacked my men, two elected deputies and …"

Again Tye did not let him finish. "Nothing makes me sicker than a man who takes another man's money to do a job and then not do it. Are they paid by the citizens of this town?"

"Si."

"Are you paid by this town?"

"Si."

"Then show these people in here that you deserve their money and do your damn job and fire those two and hire you some men who will uphold the law."

The sheriff stood up and walked out the door. A man at another table said. "Mister I don't know who you are but you just bought yourself a lot of trouble. Don't get me wrong, me and everyone in there last night saw what happened and we didn't like it but there's trouble brewing between two ranches here and most folks just want to stay out of it."

"What kind of trouble?" Sam asked acting as if he didn't know.

The man continued talking. The Masons and the Sanchez ranch are having trouble between them. Two of Sanchez's men have been murdered and Mr. Sanchez is looking at Mason who owns the lazy B as causing it."

"Why?" Tye asked thinking they may get to the bottom of this pretty dang quick.

Another man at the same table spoke to the man who had been doing the talking. "Bill, watch what you say. You don't know these men."

"I know what I saw and heard," the man called Bill said. "These men are like me, you and most everyone in here; we don't like what's going on, but don't have the balls to do or say anything and I'm tired of it. These men came in here and saw what happened, didn't like it and did something about it. Trouble is going to break out, people are going to die and personally, I don't want one or more of my family potentially being one of them."

"By opening your mouth Bill, you might just have invited yourself trouble," a man across the room stated.

"Are you threatening me, Jesse?" Bill said scooting his chair back and standing up.

"Dang it Bill," Jesse said. "We've know'd each other to long for you to say something like that and…"

Tye sensing things were heating up stood up. "Hold up a minute men. This man here," pointing at Sam, "is United States Deputy Sam Jenkins. The other man is former Deputy Bart Williams. My name is Deputy Tye Watkins and…"

Tye was interrupted this time. "From Fort Clark," another man asked.

"I was a scout there for a few years but now I'm a U.S. Marshal and Sam and I were sent down here to try and settle this problem ya'll are having." Talk was going on at every table now that everyone knew who the strangers were and most of the talk was about Tye as Sam could hear his name over and over. He smiled. Some things never change.

Sam was right, some things never change. A man came up to the table that must have been five or six inches over six foot tall. Big through the shoulders and narrow at the waist and appeared to be nothing but muscle in between. He had hair that was as black as Tye's but that is where the resemblance ended. Sam thought he was the ugliest man he ever did see and he could tell the man had trouble on his mind.

The man looked down at Tye. "Heard you were eight foot tall and could blow lightning bolts out your ass. Heard you never been whupped, that you could whup two men at a time and never break a sweat." He spit on the floor. "I think you are horseshit and all them there stories about you were made up- mostly by you."

It got suddenly very quiet in the saloon. Everyone was waiting to see what Tye would do to this man, Blake Stanley, who had bullied everyone since he came into town four or five months ago. He was a vicious fighter and had nearly beat to death a couple of the citizens of Laredo recently and had bested several of the other men who had faced him. He was not a popular figure around town.

Tye sat still. "Evidently," he said looking at Sam and then everyone else, "this young man has a problem on his hands."

"What problem do I have Mister Tye Watkins? Seems to me you have the problem just as soon as you get your ass up out of that chair."

Tye took off his hat and handed it to a smiling Sam which did not go unnoticed by Blake.

"What the hell you smiling about law dog?"

Sam took Tye's hat. "I wish I had a dollar every time some smartass youngster has tried to whip my friend here. Hell, I'd be a rich man." This brought a round of laughs from some of the men but they shut up when Blake turned and looked at them.

Tye stood up and Blake swung a right fist at his chin. Tye, expecting it stepped back and let the fist go by and knew a left was coming so he ducked it easily and slapped the man on the cheek with his open palm before Blake could regain his balance. The slap infuriated Blake and he charged like a bull buffalo. Tye stepped aside at the last instant and stuck out his foot and tripped the man. Blake hit the wooden floor hard with his face. He lay there for a moment trying to figure out what just happened. He slowly got to his feet and realized this man was toying with him so he would change his tactics and not go rushing in like a mad bull.

"This is enough Mr. .....   What's your name anyway?" Tye asked.

"I'm the sumbitch that's going to whip the famous scout from Fort Clark's ass. He feinted this time and come hard with a left that caught Tye a glancing blow on the cheek bone.   "Well youngster," Tye said, "It time you got your lesson.

Tye feinted with his right and when Blake raised his arms to block it Tye unleashed a left to the midsection that brought the arms down and then Tye let loose with a right that had all his weight behind it that lifted Blake's feet off the floor and he flew horizontally a few feet and crashed into a table splintering it. Tye walked over to look at the unconscious man and a man from the back of the room yelled.

"Is the sumbitch dead?"

A man standing near the shattered table answered. "Nah unfortunately he's still breathing."

Tye turned and walked over the bar. "On the house Tye," the bartender said handing Tye a mug of beer. "Been waiting a long time for that loudmouthed sonofabitch to get his comeuppance. Been bullying and whipping men for awhile."

"How much for the table I busted,"Tye asked reaching in his pocket.

"Well," The barkeep said rubbing his chin like he was adding up the damages.

"Way I see it you don't owe me a thing. Seems to me that cowboy over there did the damage." He walked over to the unconscious Blake and kneeling beside the big man reached in his shirt pocket and took out some money. He held it to where Tye, Sam and the others could see. "I'm taking the damages out of this." He took out five dollars and put the rest back in the man's pocket. "That seem fair to you marshals?"

Tye and Sam both nodded their heads and everyone let out a cheer.

"Round of drinks on me," a man wearing coat over a white shirt and bow string tie hollered bringing a raucous roar from the men as all dashed to the bar. The man who brought the drinks walked toward their table where the lawmen had just sat back down.

"Damn," Bart mumbled quietly. "That's Kingfisher."

"Who's Kingfisher?" Tye asked quietly.

"Tell you in a minute." Bart said.

The man reached the table and looked down at Tye and smiled. "That was something I won't forget for a long time marshal. Worth every damn penny that I'm paying for the drinks" He walked to the bar and paid the barkeep and walked out with everyone slapping him on the back.

Bart looked at Tye. "You serious about not knowing who that was?"

Tye shook his head. "Seems I've heard that name but can't place it."

"Well," Bart said leaning back in his chair and shoving the brim of his hat up. "Kingfisher was born John King Fisher, but now is known just as Kingfisher. He spent some time in the pen a few years ago and since getting out has been picked up on charges from rustling to murder but has been acquitted every time. He recently bought a ranch up north near Eagle Pass. He's reportedly rustling Texas cattle and trading them across the Border for stolen Mexican cattle. Remember what he looks like cause one of these days you will be looking for him."

Tye shook his head. "Just goes to show a person can't tell anything about a man just by looking at him. He recorded in the back of his brain what the man looked like. Sharp dresser, good looking guy with a mustache and about five foot nine and one hundred forty or so pounds with a small scar on his cheek.

At that time a man rushed in saying that another Mexican had been shot and it was one of Sanchez's nephews and the old man was pissed and reportedly gathering his men at his hacienda for a ride to Mason's ranch."

"Is there a place where we can get to where we can meet and talk to Mr. Sanchez before he gets to Masons?" Tye asked loud enough for all the men to hear.

A young cowboy stepped away from the bar. "Yessir thar is. My horse is outside and shor-nuf needs some exercise. Get your mounts and I'll be along to the livery in five minutes and we'll head out. I figure that Sanchez bunch is about to plumb burst wanting revenge so we ain't got no time to waste if'n we're going to meet them first."

Tye, Sam and Bart hustled out the door of the saloon and ran the block or so to the livery. Five minutes later the young cowboy whose name was Buster, was leading them at a fast gallop toward their meeting. After twenty minutes of hard riding they reached the place that Buster figured they could catch the men from the Sanchez ranch before they reached the Mason ranch.

"You know this Senor Sanchez Buster." Tye asked?

"Yessir I do. I called on one of his daughters for awhile."

"That could be a good deal or a bad one," Tye stated.

Buster thru his head back and laughed and when he quit laughing he said. "We're good. Nutin' ever got serious twixed us. Morn' friends than anything else."

"Good," Tye said. "When they get here we'll hold back since he don't know us and you ride out and tell him we want to talk.

Buster nodded and about that time they all heard the pounding of a lot of hooves coming toward them. Buster rode out about a hundred yards ahead of the lawmen and waited.

Chapter Five

The Sanchez riders rode almost up to Buster before reining their mount to a sliding stop and raising so much dust that the lawmen lost sight of them for a moment. A minute later the group of forty or fifty men rode easily toward them with Buster in front with a older fellow that rode with an air of authority like he was a ex officer in the Mexican army.

"Senor Sanchez rides well for an older man," Sam said.

"He was an officer with the Lancers in the Mexican army and he was decorated many times," Bart said. "He was instrumental in the Battle of Los Angeles during the Mexico war with the United States in 1846 or so. The Lancers rousted the town from a group of United States Marines."

When the two men got twenty or so yards out Tye studied the man. He definitely carried himself as man who expelled authority. He had long silver hair and neatly trimmed beard both enhanced by the rays from the sun. He wore a brightly colored Sombrero on his head and had a bandolier across his shoulder and chest with no empty loops.

Reining their mounts to a halt in front of the lawmen Buster made the introductions.

"Heard many stories about you Senor Watkins: Apache killer, lawman, and a friend to the Mexicans as well as the many settlers here in Texas. It is an honor to meet such a man."

All the men dismounted and Tye and Sanchez shook hands. "It is a honor to meet you Senor Sanchez, a man well thought of as a former Lancer officer in the

Mexican army. It is my hope that me and my friends here can get to the bottom of this trouble before any more of your men or anyone else's men are killed. How is your nephew that was shot today?"

"He will live, Senor. Thank you for asking.'

"Now can you tell us just what's going on?"

Sanchez looked around and spotted a downed tree. I am not as young as I used to be so I think I will sit on the downed tree trunk over there." All walked over to the tree and Sanchez sat down. Buster sat a few feet away from the old man on the tree also. Tye, Sam, and Bart squatted down in front of the elderly man.

"My family has been on this ranch for many years minding our own business of raising and selling sheep and running a few cattle which for the most part was to put meat on our table." He chuckled. "Most of my family including myself cannot stomach the meat from sheep." The lawmen laughed along with him.

He continued. "A couple or so years ago this man named Mason bought a ranch just northwest of Laredo-about ten thousand or so acres. He brought in too many head of cattle for what the land can support. As you have probably seen the grass here is much more sparse and shorter than the grass farther north. Things were good for awhile between us but lately not so good."

"What changed, "Sam asked?

"He told me his men told him we were stealing his cattle which I said his men were imagining things. The Sanchez Ranch runs sheep, not cattle. Anyway, one night one of my men was shot and several sheep also. I confronted Mason with the sheriff but he said none of his men were off the ranch and since there were no witnesses..."

Bart asked. "Was a fifty caliber used?"

The rancher nodded. "Si Senor. My man was shot with the heavy fifty caliber but the sheep were shot with forty-fours, probably a Winchester."

Tye asked. "How long ago was this?"

"Maybe two months ago." He hesitated for a few seconds then continued. "I had another man shot a couple days ago but the sheriff seemed to have no interest...then today my nephew was shot while watching his flock."

"I don't suppose you know who owns the land that borders Masons on the north do you?"

Sanchez nodded. "Si senor, a man named Fisher I believe."

Bart looked at Tye and Sam and smiled. "I have a good idea where Mason's cattle are going Senor Sanchez."

Tye stood up. "Yours and Mason's problems is the reason we were sent here. We will get to the bottom of this if you will give us a couple days. A couple of days is worth waiting for if it can save lives Senor Sanchez, is it not?"

Sanchez stood up. "I am a man of peace Senor Watkins. I detest killing if it can be helped. My men will be upset but they will have to do as I do...wait and see."

He stuck out his hand which Tye took in a firm handshake. "You have your two days Senor." He shook Sam's and Buck's hand and walked to his horse and mounted. The three lawmen watched him ride away and then watched as he was apparently addressing his men. They could tell they were some disagreements but in the end, all rode back the way they had come.

"I bet that sumbitch Kingfisher is responsible for Mason's cattle missing," Bart said.

"I wouldn't take that bet," Sam chuckled.

"I think it's time we visited Mr. Mason," Tye said. "I want to send a telegram first though. He asked Buster a question as they walked their horses. "Buster, what do you know about the Masons?"

"Not much Marshal. Met him a few times and he seemed alright. He shornuff has himself a good-looking filly for a wife. I've know'd his foreman, Bill Gleason for a long time and there's not a more honest cowboy anywhere. He has forgotten more about cattle than most will ever know. I know the other regular hands pretty well too. Played a lot of poker with them. Good men. The other two hands, Longley and Johnson are different folks. Don't think either knows the difference twixt a steer and a heifer."

"Which of these men carry a fifty?" Tye asked.

"Longley does."

Tye nodded and kicked Sandy slightly with his heels and they were off at a gallop.

It was mid afternoon when they rode back into Laredo and up to the telegraph office.

"Be right back," he said to the others as he dismounted and walked to the door of the telegraph office.

Entering he waited for his eyes to adjust to the dimness of the room and then walked to the man that was taking a message on the telegraph. When he was through the man looked up and asked if he could be of help.

Tye took out his badge and showed it to the agent. "I'm Deputy U.S. Marshal Tye Watkins and I need to send a telegram to our main office in San Antonio."

The small, portly man looked up at Tye and the badge. "You from Fort Clark"'

For the one thousandth time, Tye nodded as he scribbled a message on a piece of paper on the counter. I want this sent right away and I don't want to hear that you said anything to anyone about it-understood?" The last word was said with a lot of emphasis.

"Y..Yes S..Sir, Mr. Watkins," the obviously nervous little man mumbled. He took the message and read it.

It was to the U.S. Marshals Office in San Antonio asking if there were papers out on a Johnny Longley that goes by Tex or a James Johnson and to reply as soon as possible to the agent in Laredo. It was signed by Deputy Marshal Tye Watkins.

"Remember..." he looked at the name on the desk, "Not one word of this to anyone Jim. I would hate to have to come back to see you and throw your butt in jail for interfering in a investigation." He started toward the door and turned and looked over his shoulder. The clerk was still staring at him. "Send it now Jim," he said loudly." He smiled to himself as he went out the door after watching the little man scramble to the key board.

"What's so funny Tye?"

"Nothing really. You know how mouthy the clerks are that work in the telegraph offices. I just scared this one a little." He laughed again the said. "It's too late to head out to Masons today. Let's get a bite to eat and then a drink or two then get some rest. We should have an answer on the telegram by in the morning then we can head out.

After a hot meal and belling up to the bar for three or four stiff drinks Tye lay in bed thinking, trying to get a handle on this situation. He was anxious to talk to this Mason fellow and see what he's made of. Could be he's behind all this or could be he's not a part of it. If he's not then who could profit by all this. *It's been mine and Sam's experience in dealing with ranch hands they are mostly honest, hard working men who are fiercely loyal to the brand they ride for. If I was a betting man I'd put my money on this here Johnson and Longley fellows if what Buster said is true.* He smiled thinking about it. *Those two don't know the difference between a heifer and a steer. We'll know more when the telegram comes in the morning.* He turned over on his side and went to sleep.

In the morning at Big Momma's Restaurant while the three were eating a hearty breakfast the clerk from the telegraph office brought the message they were waiting for. Tye took the telegram and read it and then handed it to Sam and said.

"Looks like our two friends at the Masons are a couple of tough characters."

Bart asked. "Something in that telegram?"

Sam handed the telegram to Bart whose eyes got wide as he read it. "You two should have shot them two varmints yesterday when you had the chance."

Tye nodded and reread the telegram from his boss in San Antonio. Seems the two men have been involved in several killings but were all supposedly justifiable as self defense-all but one. Seems that the man named Longley is wanted in New Mexico for shooting a man in the back from ambush and the gun used was a big fifty caliber. The two men had an argument that day and as the man returned to a small ranch he owned he was cut down. No witnesses but Longley was the only man around that anyone knew of that had a fifty. Circumstance put the blame on him and he confirmed it by quickly leaving the area.

"Let's go see this Mason feller and see if he can prove to us he isn't involved in this debacle."

"Debacle," Sam exclaimed. "Where in hell did you come up with that term?"

"Heard Rebecca use it a few times." Tye chuckled.

"Whal, I be hornswaggled if'n I know what it means," Bart said.

Sam answered laughing. "It means trouble in this case. We wonder if he is involved in this trouble."

"Oh," Bart said looking a little sheepish.

Tye slapped him on the shoulder. "Don't worry about it pard. I didn't know either till Rebecca explained it to me. "Let's take a ride out to Mason's and see if we can get to the bottom of all this."

Chapter Six

The three men took a leisurely ride to the Mason ranch. It was a forty-five minute ride and even Tye, not being a cowman, could see there were too many cattle for this land of sparse short grass and as far as he knew the only water being the Rio Grande River which formed the western boundary of the ranch. As they rode into the yard they saw a modest ranch house made of adobe with a wooden roof covered in mud and grass. There was a similar building they figured was the bunkhouse, a corral and a three-sided building connected to the corral they figured was too keep the horses dry when it rained as well as a tack room. The open side faced the south so when the colder winter wind blew from the north they horses were protected. There were a dozen or so horses in the corral. Everything looked well kept.

As they rode into the yard a man stepped out of the house with a rifle. "That's far enough. Who are you and what can I do for you."

A man with a rifle asking that question was not unusual out here where so many desperados ride the range so the three were not surprised.

"We are U.S. Marshals and would to sit down with you and palaver some if your name is Mason."

"Ya'll got names?"

Tye smiled. "Yes sir we do. My name is Tye Watkins and this here ugly fellow is Sam Jenkins and the man there is Bart Williams. Okay if we step down?"

"That's fine. Coffee's on so come on in." Tye noticed the barrel of the rifle drop a little but still was handy for a quick shot if needed.

As they dismounted Sam noticed the barrel and whispered, "Trusting soul ain't he?

"Folks out here live longer being that way," Tye whispered back.

Sam was shocked that the rancher hadn't mentioned Tye and Fort Clark which was one of the rare times that had happened when Tye introduced himself. As they sat down at the table the rancher asked.

"You the Watkins feller from up at Fort Clark," Mason inquired. Sam almost choked on his coffee when he laughed.

"Did I say something funny," Mason asked?

"No, no," Sam said. "It's just I thought you was one of the few men in Texas who hadn't heard the stories about this ugly galoot." He laughed again.

"I must say that the stories I've heard were a little hard to believe, at least some of them anyway."

Tye started to say something but Sam cut him off. "Been riding with him for over two years now and seen some things myself that were pretty damn amazing. I know a lot of the troopers including a Captain McClelland and the Post Commander Major Thurston. All of them said the stories about this man were true and there was a hell of lot more that people don't know and hadn't heard because no man would believe them."

"For instance," Mason asked.

"Well, let's see," Sam said rubbing his chin. "There was the time the patrol he was scouting for got themselves ambushed and trapped in a canyon with no way out, at least not on horses. They were in real trouble. That night Tye snuck out of the canyon on foot, killed a couple of Apache guards and ran the thirty-five or forty miles to Clark on foot. He led, without rest, a troop of Calvary back and rescued the trapped patrol."

"Forty miles," an astonished Mason said.

San nodded. "I could tell you more Mr. Mason but we're on official business."

"Oh," he said. Then what can I do for you?"

About that time all the men stood up as one of the prettiest ladies Sam ever saw walked into the room with a tray of coffee mugs and each man took a cup each thanking her. She left as quick as she had come in.

"That was my wife Linda. She's a little shy around strangers. Now what can I do for you," he said as they all sat down. Sam stared at the door the lady had went through for a second before sitting down.

"Yesterday," Tye said. "We stopped about forty or more men coming to you ranch from the Sanchez's ranch led by Senor Sanchez himself."

Mason looked startled. "Why would he be coming here?"

Sam answered. "I do believe they were going to kill you and your men."

Mason sit his mug down so hard some spilled on his hand, burning him. "Damn," he said. "But why would they be coming here to do that? I've lost a few cattle but not enough to start a war.

The three lawmen looked at other and each knew this man did not have a clue. Tye cleared his throat. "How long as it been since you have been in town?"

"I don't know, maybe two months or so. Linda loves it here and isn't much of a social person and I don't like to leave her here by herself. One of the men goes into town for our supplies."

"You have a Johnny Longley and James Johnson working here on the ranch," Tye said in more of a question than a statement.

Mason nodded. "I have a James Johnson and a Tex Longley, " Mason answered. "They ride the range trying to catch the cattle thieves."

"You know anything about them," Bart asked.

"Not when I hired them. I was losing a few head according to my foreman and I mentioned it to J.T.

Brimley and he suggested I hire a couple of men to see if they could put a stop to it."

"Who is this J.T. Brimley?" Tye asked. His suspicion rising.

"He's my banker."

Tye nodded. "How did you come across those two men you hired?"

Mr. Brimley recommended them to me. Is there anything wrong? What's this all about?"

A picture of what was going on flashed immediately across each of the lawmen's brains. Each of them had seen it before. Trouble between ranchers, men killed, a rancher not wanting to endanger his family any longer is killed and the widow selling out cheap.

Tye laid out what had been going on to Mason; the killing and wounding of Sanchez men, the slaughter of sheep, and the harassment of Sanchez's men in town.

"What makes you think my men had anything to do with it?"

"We had a run in with them the night we rode into Laredo. They were fixing to beat the hell out a one of Sanchez's men who could not have weighed more than one hundred and forty or so pounds. We stepped in and put a stop to it and almost had a shoot out with them."

"They got smart real quick when they started to draw their guns and were suddenly looking at the wrong end of two Colts pointed at them." Bart chuckled. "They dropped their gun belts and then Tye here," he laughed. "He taught the big one a lesson he won't forget. He beat the hell out of him and never even got touched by the sumbitch. "

"Fighting someone is long ways from killing a man."

"Yes sir it is," Tye replied. "I have a telegram from San Antonio that is from the U.S. Marshal saying that Tex is wanted in New Mexico for killing a man, shot him in the back. The weapon used was a big fifty caliber Sharps. Not too many of those around. He has killed other men also but in what was called a fair fight. The Sanchez men were killed with a fifty caliber Sharps."

"Who was those men that rode in," Tex asked James who was looking out the bunkhouse window.

"Those men who were in the saloon that night that we hassled that mex. The one who you fought with is one of them. Think I saw one of the flash a badge to Mason"

"Grab your things and let's get the hell out of here now," Tex said has he filled his saddle bag with shirts and extra shells for his big fifty."

"Why?"

"I'd bet my last dollar those bastards are marshals and they have figured things out."

"What about our pay?"

"If you want yours bad enough go see Mason now but I'm out of here. He was out the door and in the corral and saddling his horse. He was out of the corral and waiting on James when the door to the ranch house opened and Mason stepped out and hollered their names and told them to come to the house. Without thinking, Tex raised the Sharps and fired. Mason was blown by the force of the heavy lead back into the house. He reined his mount around and headed east as fast as he horse would run.

James came out of the house just as Tye stuck his head out of the ranch house door. Tye hollered for him to drop his gun belt, but James still not grasping the situation went for his gun. He had barely cleared leather when Tye's bullet hit him just above the belt buckle. He grasped his belly with both hands and fell to the ground.

"Take care of Mason Buck, the other one is getting away," Tye hollered as he ran to the bunkhouse house with Sam on his heels. They reached the fallen man and Tye knelt down and rolled him over. James's eyes fluttered and then opened.

Tye said. "You're done James. Nobody but God can help you now."

James looked up and grimaced and said through clinched teeth. "Don't reckon He gives a damn about me. W...would like to kno...know who shot me though" he said struggling to say anything.

"He cares for all of us James." Tye whispered and placed his hand under the man's head and lifted it up some. "Just ask him for forgiveness and let him into your heart."

He nodded his head a mumbles some words and a small sign of a smile crossed his face and then relaxed in death.

Sam came up with their horses and Tye mounted Sandy and started out after Tex knowing it was going to be dangerous hunting a man that can shoot a fifty as well as he can and knowing the gun can kill at such a long distances. *Makes a man's hair stand up on the back of his neck Tye thought.* He smiled. He loved it.

Chapter Seven

"He ain't going far if he keeps running that horse of his like he is," Tye hollered at Sam. They were at a fast gallop which a good horse like each of them had could hold for a good spell.

Twenty minutes later Tye pointed to the ground. "He's starting to flounder. That bastard is going to kill his horse." He slowed Sandy down to a trot. Better be on the lookout now. With that dang Sharps he can shoot a half mile way and he's obviously he is pretty good with that big gun."

"How far behind him are we?"

'"Close enough to be real careful. His horse is stumbling now so I figure he'll go down within a mile. Keep a sharp eye Sam. Watch for any movement or the sun reflecting on something. Be ready to get out of the saddle." Both men pulled their Henry's from the saddle scabbard and kicked their feet out of the stirrups.

Fifteen minutes later Tye reined in. A horse lay fifty or so yards ahead of them. "It's going to get real interesting now Sam."

"Dammed Tye," Sam said dismounting. "I always hate it when you say that because it means someone's gonna die."

"Let's just make sure it's not one of us partner, "Tye said giving Sam a big grin.

I *honestly think that when times like this comes along and I'm about to piss in my pants he is actually enjoying this, sorter like it's a damn game to him,* Sam thought to himself.

An instant later Tye shoved Sam hard enough to throw him to the ground and Tye hit the ground also. A bullet shattered the trunk of a mesquite and a second later the boom of the big fifty. Sam looked at the split trunk of the mesquite and figured it was just about where his chest would have been.

"Seen the glint of sunlight on something on that hill about a quarter mile over yonder," Tye said pointing with the barrel of his Henry rifle. He's about thirty or so yards from the top of the hill in that cluster of cedars and rocks. He picked a bad spot if you look at things. It's open ground above him and to his right so he only has two ways to go if wants to run."

"How we gonna flush him out?"

"I'm working on that." Tye studied the lay of the land all around him then said. "Sam, you stay here and make sure he doesn't go over the top or to his right. I'm gonna injun down this shallow wash and see I can get to his left and then we'll see if we can get him to surrender when he realizes we have him in a crossfire." Sam nodded and laid the barrel of his rifle on a rock to steady his aim if he had to fire.

Tye got into the wash which was only a couple feet deep with a sandy bottom. He begin bellying his way down the wash moving slow so has not to raise any dust. There was no sound, no birds chirping, no rustle of small animals and even the slight breeze seemed to lay down making it stifling hot. Then he heard a sound he didn't want to hear; the distinct sound of a rattler warning him to stay away.

He raised his head slightly and spotted the snake about four feet in front of him under the lip if the wash and in the shade of a large boulder. He raised himself up enough to look over the edge of the wash to see exactly where he was. He was past the clump of cedars where the shooter was or at least was fifteen minutes ago if he hadn't moved to his left away from where Sam could have seen him. He would worry about the shooter in a minute but right now he had a more pressing problem.

The rattler was in a striking position with his head above his coiled body and back in the infamous S position, ready to strike. His unblinking eyes stared straight into Tye's sending shivers up Tye's spine. The never-ending buzz of his rattlers were extremely loud in the confines of the narrow wash. Sweat ran down Tye's face and neck soaking his shirt.

Tye had been carrying his rifle in the crook of his arms as he crawled along the wash. He took the Henry by the barrel and raising his body slightly pressed the butt of the Henry against the rattler pinning him under the rock. He held pressure on the snake and worked his body past the venomous reptile and then took the rifle from the snake's body and felt the blow on the butt of the gun as the rattler struck viciously at the object hurting him. Tye scrambled quickly away wanting no part of a second encounter. He noticed the broken fang in the rifles butt and surrounded by a wet spot where the venom sprayed. He took his Bowie from his boot and cut the fang away and using sand wiped the venom off.

He crawled another ten yards or so and stopping took his hat off and looked over the rim of the wash. No sign of Tex but farther study where the outlaw was revealed good news to the lawman. Another wash, this one appeared wider and deeper ran down the side of the hill having been cut out of the rock and dirt by water coming down from above over hundreds of years. He found where it ran into the wash he was in and started to go up the hill in it but stopped.

Boot prints in the sand, recent ones, and no more than a few minutes old. Tye swore under his breath and looked farther up the wash he had been in and immediately dropped to his belly and rolled into the wash coming down the hill. A bullet cut a gash across the back of his calf.

"Damn," he said out loud as the burning in his leg was like someone laid a hot poker across the back of his leg. He looked at his leg and saw it wasn't serious but that didn't keep it from hurting like hell. He then thought, *At least it's my leg and not my head which it would have been if I hadn't seen Tex just before he pulled the trigger. There's good in everything I guess.* He took his kerchief and pulling his pants leg up, wrapped it tightly around his calf. *Didn't help with the pain none but maybe it will keep some of the dirt out of it,* he thought.

This situation which was bad now just got a hell of lot worse, Tye thought. *He's on foot and will be able to lay up anywhere and pick me or Sam or both of us off if we make a mistake.* He took a quick look where Tex had been but saw nothing. He took a longer look and seeing no sign of the man stood up and started limping toward where Sam was.

"Don't shoot Sam," he hollered when he was close enough to be heard. He saw Sam stand up and come towards him. Noticing the limp Sam asked.

"I heard the big gun. You hit?"

"Yeah, but it's just a scratch, nothing serious."

"Let's take a look at it while you fill me in on what happened." Tye sat down and pulled his pants leg up. Sam undid the kerchief from the wound. "Damn man, I thought you said it was just a scratch. The dang thing is a quarter inch deep."

Tye said. Can you get me a clean shirt from my saddle bags and there's a bottle of rot gut in there too."

Sam came back with the shirt and bottle. "Pour a little on the wound Sam."

"It's a waste of good whiskey," Sam chuckled. He poured some on the wound and Tye let out with some cuss words that shocked Sam.

A minute later Tye had cut a strip from the clean shirt and Sam wrapped his leg with it. This is going to be tough Sam," Tye said. "He's on foot and I noticed his canteen is still on his horse so he's gonna be desperate in a short while. He's going to be hungry, thirsty, and madder than hell and he's going to want nothing more than to kill us."

"So, what's different about this man than the dozens of others we have brought in? They sure as hell wanted us dead too."

"Nothing other than the fact he has a gun that can kill a man from a quarter of a mile or more away. We, my friend, are going to have to be dang careful tracking this one down so let's get started." He stood up and tested his leg. It was a little painful but not so a man could not stand it. They walked to their horses and taking the reins in their left hand and carrying their rifle in their right, started off on what Tye figured was his most dangerous hunt of all. Two hours later they picketed their horses and sat down to eat some jerky and drink a little water. They had taken the canteen from Tex's horse and some biscuits from his saddle bags. With each of them carrying two canteens and this extra one water would be no problem-at least for a day or so.

"We close?"

Tye looked around. "Hopefully we not in his sights right now."

Sam choked on a piece of jerky, "That close huh?" Tye nodded.

"Reason I stopped I got a glimpse of sun light reflecting off something and since not many things in nature reflect light I figure he found himself a hole and is waiting." He looked up at the sun. It's about three or so now so it's going to get a lot warmer than it is now. I thought we would make him wait a little. He might just make a mistake if he gets thirsty enough. Been there before myself and things can get a little fuzzy in your head when you go a long stretch with nothing to drink and the sun bearing down on you."

"Where's he at?" Sam questioned after looking at his pocket watch and shaking his head. It was ten minutes till three.

"About a half mile ahead. The reflection was about half way up the side of a hill. He's no pilgrim at ambushing so I figure he found a place he feels safe and has a good field of fire. The only disadvantage he has is that big fifty he's using is a single shot and take three or four seconds to eject the shell and put another in the chamber and close it. A man can cover a lot of ground in three or four seconds."

"I agree with your thinking and it makes sense-if he misses you with the first shot."

"We'll just have to make sure he does." Tye chuckled and slapped his friend on the shoulder. "Let's go flush him out."

"Hold on a minute. I need to empty my bladder before it busts."He walked a few steps away and took care of his business. "Let's go get the sonofbitch."

Chapter Eight

Thirty minutes later after leaving the horses and walking, crawling and using every bit of cover they could find Tye felt they were below where he saw the flash of sun light about seventy-five yards above them. The hill wasn't as steep as Tye thought it might be and actually looked as if the rocky ground was solid enough to where a man would not be slipping a sliding going up it. Tye studied the area where he figured Tex to be. He saw nothing at first but then he saw a branch of a cedar move then he realized it was not a branch but a long barrel of a rifle sticking out of the cedar.

"He's there Sam. I saw the barrel of his fifty sticking out of the cedars. This is going to be a little tricky but here's what we need to do unless you have a better plan."

"I'm listening."

"Make sure you have a full load in your Henry. I want you to fire as many shots as you can to keep his head down while I move up the hill. I'm leaving my rifle with you so you have plenty firepower. When I get to my spot I will signal you again to start firing till I get to the next and so own. Okay?"

"No it don't Tye. It's a good plan but with your leg I need to be the one moving up the hill, not you."

Tye thought about it for a moment and it made sense that Sam could move a hell of lot better than him. "Okay partner but know where you are going before you take off." Sam nodded his head and they shook hands and looked at each with a understanding that this could be the last time one of them sees the other till the hereafter.

Tye said. "See the large boulder just about twenty yards up and slightly to your right. That's your first stop and the clump of cedars twenty yards or so farther up is your second. After that you pick them out." Sam nodded his understanding. Tye worked the lever and injected a shell into the chamber. When you are ready Sam just go.

A second later Sam took off and immediately Tye begin firing where he saw the barrel a few minutes ago. He had fired ten shells when Sam reached the first spot. Tye picked up his Henry and jacked a shell into the chamber and waited for Sam to take off.

Sam took off and Tye fired into the cedars and then saw a movement to the left of Sam and a quick glance showed a man standing up and bringing his rifle to bear on Sam. Just as he fired Sam, seeing the shooter threw himself to the ground. Tye swung his Henry and fired a second after the man did. Tye didn't miss. Tex threw the rifle in the air screaming in pain and fell to the ground and begin rolling down the hill. Tye followed him with the Henry to make sure he didn't get up. When it was apparent he wasn't he rushed to his friend to check on him.

Sam was on his side and in obvious pain. "Where you hit," Tye screamed as he got within a few feet of his friend.

"I think he blew my ass off," Sam said through gritted teeth. "Damn and double Damn."

Seeing Sam wasn't fatally shot he said. "Just lie there partner while I check on that back shooting bastard. He scrambled down the hill with his pistol in his hand to where Tex lay. The man was moving his legs and moaning. Tye, making sure he had nothing in his hands rolled him over on his back. His bullet had hit him high in the shoulder just under the collar bone and exited out the back. Not a fatal wound but dang painful. He hand cuffed Tex's hands behind his back which Tye knew was painful with the shoulder wound and then tied his feet securely. This done he scrambled back up the hill to check on Sam.

'You need to stand up and drop them pants so I can see how bad it is Sam. Sam stood up as best he could. The seat of his pants and one pants leg was soaked in blood. Sam undid his pants and dropped them. Tye took his Bowie and cut the bottom of his long johns out.

"H..ho..how bad is it Tye? Damn it hurts."

"Not as much now as it will when I pour that rotgut on your butt," Tye said laughing.

"Damn you man, I'm hurting." Tye laughed even louder. "It's not funny you sonofabitch so quit laughing."

"You'll live partner but you ain't going to sit a horse for awhile," he chuckled. "The bullet cut a gash across both cheeks of your butt about like the one on my leg. Painful but not serious unless it gets infected and you have to have both cheeks amputated," Tye said chuckling.

If looks could kill Tye would be dead. "You mean by ass ain't gone."

"I just told you it wasn't serious, just painful." Sam smiled, then grimaced. "Let me carry you down to the bottom of the hill and then I will get our prisoner."

"He ain' t dead"

"He's hit hard but he'll live to hang."

He may not live to hang because I may shoot the sonofabitch for shooting me in the ass."

Tye smiled at that last remark and walked, or limped, over to Tex. Tye reached down and jerked him to his feet and Tex screamed in pain. "Let's go over to my partner you piece of shit. I think he may just shoot you for shooting him in the butt." Tye untied his feet and led him to where Sam waited.

Tye made a travois and then tended to Sam's wound which, when he poured whiskey on his butt Sam did his best to out cuss any man alive using words Tye never heard before. Sam apologized when it quit burning.

Tye got Sam on the travois laying him on his side. He walked over to Tex and squatted in front of him. "Who put you up to all this Tex?"

"Up to what?"

I know you shot those Mexicans that worked for Sanchez and that your partner shot the sheep. I'm just wondering why you would take money for killing men."

Tex said nothing, just staring off in the distance.

Tye figured he had to gamble. "What did J.T. Brimley promise you and James?"

Tex jerked his head around and looked at Tye. "What makes you think he promised anything to us. He jus..." he stopped short realizing he was confessing. "I don't know what you are talking about."

Tye realized he had nailed his suspension down just said. "Don't matter anyway what you say now because either you or J.T. will talk sooner or later."

The travois was behind Sandy so Tye walked over to get Sam's horse for Tex to ride.

Sam whispered to Tex. "I don't give a damn about you but I'm going to give you a little advice, but first do you know who that man is?"

"Just another stinking law dog."

"That's Tye Watkins, the Apache killer from Fort Clark. He's more Apache than white when he's mad. I've seen what he can do to a man to get information and it ain't pretty. Mostly, he uses that big Bowie of his. He can put a lot of pain to a man without killing him, only making the man wish he was dead. If'n he ask you another question I would think twice about not answering him."

Tye came back leading Sam's horse. "I was just telling Tex here about how good you were with that knife when you got mad." He gave Tye a wink.

Catching on to what Sam meant Tye pulled his Bowie with the ten inch blade on the ground in front of Tex and starting to gather a few sticks."

"Whatcha doing Watkins?"

"Building a fire and going to have me some fun, Apache style. He picked up the Bowie and shaved some hair off his arm. That should do fine Sam."

"Can you roll me over so I don't have to watch? Last time I was sick for a week. You damned Apaches are a sick people," Sam said playing the role to the hilt.

"Y...you ca..can't do this. You're a lawman."

Tye turned Sam over to face the other direction and proceeded to build a fire. "Don't appear to be anyone around Tex. Who will know?"

'Okay. What do you want to know?"

"What did J.T. promise you and James?"

"If his plan worked a thousand dollars each plus a hundred dollar bonus for every Mexican of Sanchez's killed."

"What was his plan?"

"Don't know. He never said. James and me figured he would buy the ranch cheap if Mason ended up being killed and his widow would want to sell and move back to where ever she came from. I think he knew Sanchez would wipe him out or maybe Sanchez and his kin would be killed and his ranch would be put up for sale."

"Can you write?"

'Hell yes. I'm not ignorant."

"I'm going to get Sam to write down what you just told me and then you are going to sign it. " He picked up his Bowie and flipped it in his hand to where he held it by the blade. He flicked his wrist and the Bowie stuck in the trunk of a mesquite about a foot from Tex's head before the outlaw even knew he had thrown it. Okay?"

Tex looked at the knife and nodded his head.

Sam wrote down what he had confessed to and had him sign it. Tye got Tex on Sam's horse and tied his hands to the saddle horn, mounted Sandy and headed back to Laredo.

Gary McMillan

Chapter Nine

Arriving back in Laredo they attracted quite a crowd as Tye rode down the street with Sam on a Travois and Tex barely staying in the saddle and blood all over his shirt in front and back. A weary Tye reined in front of the sheriff's office and Bart came out.

"Need the doc Bart." Tye said dismounting. As he did everyone saw the blood on his pants leg and then the limp as he walked up the steps where Bart was and shook his friends hand.

"One of you men go get the doc and be damn quick about it," Bart said then added. "Two of you help Sam off that travois and into my office and put him on the cot. You two," he said pointing to two ranch hands standing close by," get that piece of shit off that horse and in here and put him in a cell."

"I need a doctor."

"You'll get a doctor when he is finished with these two and not before."

Tye asked. 'How's Mason?"

"He'll live but he's going to need some rest for awhile."

Tye handed the piece of paper to Bart that Tex's confession was signed on. Bart read it.

"I'll be back in a minute."Bart said. He walked down the street to the bank and straight into Brimley's office.

"You can't just come storming in here," J.T. said standing up from his desk. As he did he caught a right fist square on the chin knocking him across the room and into a bookshelf spilling books and making a hell of a lot of noise. One of the clerks came running in and saw his boss unconscious on the floor.

"Wh..Whats going on?"

"What's your name son," Bart asked?

"Mike, Mike Walters."

"Well Mike, I think you just got a promotion since your horseshit boss here is under arrest for conspiracy to commit murder." He walked over to Brimley and jerked him to his feet after slapping him a few times to wake him up. He looked at Mike. "You'd had better run a honest bank here or I'll come get you. Understand?"

"Yes sir."

Bart dragged the banker across the street and into the jail where he threw him in the cell next to Tex.

The doctor had finished with Sam and was working on Tye when Tye asked. "Any trouble Bart?"

"Naw," Bart said. "He did slip and hit his chin on the desk though."

Tye laughed. "I think I'll get a bath and into some clean clothes. How about you Sam?"

"How in hell can I get into a tub with my ass wrapped in bandages?' They all laughed except Sam.

The doc said. "I have a very nice looking your lady working for me. I bet she would help you with your bath and bandages." He looked at Tye and winked.

"Well now. That sounds like a great idea to me," Sam said laughing.

"Is Charlie still around town," Tye asked to no one in particular.

"I seen him about an hour ago playing poker at the saloon," Bart said. As if on cue Charlie struck his head in the office door.

"Come over Charlie" Tye said. "I was just asking about you and wonder if you could do us one more favor?"

"Shor nuff, Tye. What is it?"

Ride out to Sanchez's and ask him to meet me at Mason's ranch tomorrow about noon and we'll get all this trouble straightened out."

"Yes sir. I'm on my way."

For the first time Tye noticed the sheriff's badge on Barts chest. "You the sheriff here now?"

Bart nodded. "Temporally till they can hire a good man."

"Well, they got one now so good luck. I'm going to get that bath and sleep for a week. Maybe by that time my partner's butt will be well enough to go home." Everyone laughed.

Gary McMillan

Tye Watkins

In

Comanche War Cry

Chapter One

Tye and Sam had been ordered to San Angelina (later named San Angelo) to see about a bank robbery where several townsfolk had been gunned down. The sheriff, James Teague, had wired the Marshals' office in San Antonio about the robbery and killings. If it had been by mail the letter would not even have arrived in San Antonio for a week or more and then a few more days in getting to the town. Thanks to the telegraph Tye and Sam would get there only four days later instead of probably two weeks.

After four hard days of riding the lawman sat on their horses on a small hill just south of the town. "Damn if I don't think this is the exact spot we sat looking at Fort Concho and San Angelina about two months ago," Sam muttered.

"Yep!' Tye answered. " I hope this time doesn't lead to the problems we had last time," he said referring to when they had been here before chasing Jed Summers or *El Diablo* as he had liked to be called.

"It would be nice to have a simple case after the last two we had for sure," Sam said agreeing. "But Like said before, riding with you is never going be easy since we both know you get the toughest. Both men nudged their mounts into a trot toward the town and Fort Concho.

They rode up to the sheriff's office and dismounted. Several of the locals were pointing at them and whispering to their friends as they were dismounting obviously some remembering them from the last time they were here.

Just as they stepped on the porch the office door opened and Sheriff Teague walked out and greeted them.

"Great to see you two again," he said shaking their hands. "Come on in and have a drink and wash some of the trail dust down and I'll fill you in on the robbery."

Inside the spotless office the three sat down around the desk and Teague poured each a drink and set the bottle to where all could reach it. "Before we get the current robbery tell me about "El Diablo". I know you ended up killing him way down south at Eagle Pass.

"Ain't a lot to tell Sheriff," Tye said, "except he killed people all the way to Eagle Pass where we caught up with him. He wounded Sam and I shot him and he was in jail when a twister hit the town and he escaped when the jail was pretty well demolished. He killed a deputy in the escape. I tracked him south and we had a hell of a fight with knives and he cut me a little before I killed him."

"Cut you a little like hell," Sam said. "He had passed out from loss of blood and damn near dead when Sandy brought him back into Eagle Pass."

"Well thank God you are okay and he is dead and gone to his reward which I'm sure is a nice warm place," he said smiling while pouring another round of drinks.

"What happened here," Sam asked?

"Some tough looking hombres rode into town about a week ago. You know the type, guns tied down and looked like they had been used a lot. Rode horses that were a hell of lot better stock than the average cowboy would ride. There were all tough looking and you could tell they weren't afraid of nothing. I knew they were trouble when I saw them in the saloon but I couldn't do a dang thing since they were breaking no laws. I looked at all the posters in my office but could not find any papers out on them."

They had rooms at the hotel and were here for two days before they pulled the job at the bank.

"How many were there," Tye asked.

"Not sure because they never all sat together or mingled together. They rode in two or so at a time over a day and a half. I think there were at least seven of them.

When they hit the bank they had two men lounging on the porch of the last business on the north road. That's the direction they headed after the robbery. The two opened up a covering fire as the others left the bank and headed out of town. They killed two men in the bank, a teller and a local merchant. The two men on the porches I told you about killed three more and wounded four merchants and cowboys as they come outside to see what was going on. Those two were hell on wheels with a rifle. We, my posse and me, chased them for a day and a half before giving up."

"They were headed north," Tye questioned. "Ain't that Comanche country-Quanah Parker's country?"

"Sure as hell is," Teague replied. "That's the main reason we came back. Ain't no white man safe in that part of Texas. Even the patrols from Fort Concho don't go very far in the country north of here."

"Any particular things about any of the men that stand out like scars and such," Sam asked.

"The man who was apparently the leader or at least that's what the banker told me was a big man, over six foot and maybe two hundred pounds. He had a scar that ran from his left eyebrow to the corner of his mouth which may his mouth sorter curl up in a sneer on that side."

"Can we talk to this banker,"Tye asked?

"Sure can. Let's go."

It was a short walk to the bank and the first thing Tye noticed was the stains on the wooden floor. They walked directly to of office of the bank president.

The banker stood up from behind his desk when the lawmen entered. "What can I do for you Sheriff?"

Mr. Farabee, these men here are U.S. Marshals sent here to see if they can track down the men who robbed your bank. This is Tye Watkins and Sam Jenkins."

Mr. Farabee said with a smile as he shook Tye's hand. "Well Mr. Watkins, if you are even close to your reputation as a tracker I figure those men are in a lot of trouble.

"We're going to give it our best shot,"" Tye replied.

"Mr. Farabee," Sam said. "Sheriff Teague said you noted that the apparent leader of this group had a scar from the corner of his left eyebrow to the corner of his mouth that caused his upper lip to stay in a permanent sort of snarl."

"Yes sir and a most unpleasant fellow I might say. He almost beat one of my tellers to death with his pistol and then shot two of my customers because they were a little slow in taking their money out of their pockets."

"You know this man Sam?" Tye asked knowing Sam had seen and heard of a lot more outlaws than he had.

"I think so and if I'm right we are in for a damn dangerous chase."

Tye looked at him for a moment. "Well?"

"I pray to God I'm wrong," Sam answered. "Mr. Farabee, did this man walk with a limp?"

"Well yes now that I think about it. He did. His right leg appeared to be a little shorter than his right."

"Damn!" Sam exclaimed.

"Who is he, Sam?"

"Jesse Lambert. He was captured after a fight with a posse three years ago in east Texas. Was shot four times but lived somehow. I thought he was hung when he recovered from his wounds. Apparently not."

"We can send a wire to San Antonio to find out," Teague said.

"Do it sheriff," Tye said. Teague rushed out the door.

"Tell me about this Lambert fellow Sam."

'Let's have a seat," Sam said. After they had sat down Sam started. "Jesse was nineteen when he first got into trouble in Fort Worth. His folks had a small farm and he didn't cotton to hard work which it took on a farm. He and his dad had a falling out and he left home and was continually in trouble for petty things, picking pockets and fighting mostly. Five years ago it escalated. He fell in with a gang and began committing robberies and a couple men got killed."

The best we can figure out he and the gang leader got into it and Jesse beat the hell out of him and then stabbed him to death. The man he killed had a reputation as a bad ass so the other members didn't say much when Jesse took over. After that it was robbery after robbery and a killing or killings on almost every one of them. It was reported by a gang member that got himself caught and told a lot about the going on within the gang before he got himself hung. He said Jesse had killed two of his gang for back talking to him. Jesse and every one of the gang know if they are caught they face a hanging so they ain't going to be anxious to give themselves up."

"Whew, I see what you mean Pard. This could be tough and on top of that we have the Comanche to worry about if they keep going north. We'll hang around and get some supplies while waiting on the telegraph message from headquarters and maybe we will find out this man is not Jesse."

"Sheriff," Tye said, "Can you direct us to the general store?"

"Course...course I can." He got up from his chair and started out the door with the lawmen following. Outside the bank he pointed south and said. "The store is two blocks down on this side of the street. A Mr. Briggs is the proprietor."

"Thanks for your help Mr. Farabee," Tye said shaking the bankers hand he and Sam walked down the street to Mr. Briggs store.

"There it is," Sam said pointing to the store just across the street with the big sign GENERAL STORE on it. Entering the store both men were struck by how well stocked it was.

"Damn,"Sam said. "I bet there aint't nothing a man could want that ain't here somewhere.

Tye nodded his agreement and they started gathering the things they needed: shells for their Colts and Henrys, jerky, coffee, sugar, beans, and a pound of bacon. Everything would fit in their saddle bags so they would not need a packhorse that would need water and probably slow them down. They had five canteens between them for their selves and the horses. They knew water was scarce except for the Concho River and farther north the Colorado River and west, the Pecos, but both knew they may not always be near any of them depending on where the outlaws went.

As they came out of the store a lieutenant with a couple of privates met them. The lieutenant introduced himself.

"Mt name is Lieutenant John Dixon," he said sticking out his hand to Tye. Being much bigger than Sam, he added. "I take it you are Tye Watkins. Tye nodded shaking the man's hand. 'And you must be Sam Jenkins," he said reaching for Sam's hand.

"The major at the fort would like to see both of you right away if you don't mind," then added with a smile. "It was more of an order than a request."

"Any idea of what he wants us for," Sam asked?

"No sir, but he sure has a burr up his butt about something," he chuckled.

A few minutes later they walked into the fort headquarters and into the major's office.

After saluting, the Lieutenant introduced Tye and Sam to Major Tinsley. The major excused the lieutenant who left the office.

"It's an honor to meet the both of you," he said. "I've been keeping up with you thru the newspapers and every once in awhile, the telegraph. Quite an impressive thing you are doing to help rid this country of varmints" He motioned to the chairs. "Have a seat."

"I guess you both are wondering why I sent for you." Tye and Sam nodded. "One of the men killed by those men who robbed the bank was my son-in-law. He and my daughter had been married a year and was expecting their first child in a couple of months. I know this is not army business but I'm using this as an excuse to send a troop north to scout the country and find where this Quannah Parker is camped but I haven't sent one as of yet."

"Why not Major," Tye asked. "From what I seen coming over here you have a hell of lot of men."

Major Tinsley nodded his head. "And not one damn scout I can trust. I've heard stories about you every since I came out here Tye and I feel this is the time."

"We're chasing outlaws Major," Sam said. "Not looking for Indians."

"And besides, I don't know the country north of here, never been there," Tye said.

"I realize that Tye. I said I didn't have a scout I could trust, not that I don't have any that doesn't know the land. They don't know Indians like you do. I know you are after the men who robbed the bank and that will be your main objective but while you are out there the scout and the troops can be looking for Indian signs and will not be in your way. I will instruct the lieutenant you just met, Mr. Dixon, that you will be in charge and all his orders must go through you. He is young but very capable."

Tye thought about it for a moment then nodded. "Okay on one condition."

"What's the condition?"

"The troops remove the crossed swords emblem off their hats and anything else that might reflect sun light including the swords of the officers. That it is understood Sam and me are in charge and any orders we give will be followed immediately without question. When I was scouting at Clark that was understood by the men and officers. It can mean the difference between life and death sometimes if I don't have to explain things or argue with an officer."

"I will take care of that Mr. Watkins."

"When can your men be ready to go?"

"I took the liberty of having a twenty man patrol ready now," Tinsley answered. "I will have them remove the items you talked about and anything else that might make noise or reflect sunlight. I will tell the officers in front of the men that what you or Sam says is to be treated as if an officer gave the command."

"Fair enough Major. Let's get to it then."

Ten minutes later the troop was assembled in front of headquarters with Major Tinsley addressing the men.

"Men, these two gentlemen on my right are U.S. Marshals and are in pursuit of the men who robbed the bank. The big fellow is Tye Watkins that scouted at Fort Clark for years and also Sam Jenkins who has made quite a reputation for himself as a lawman. You will go with them and while looking for the outlaws look for signs that might lead us to Quanah Parker and his camp. Their orders are to be carried out without question. Is that understood?"The men nodded their heads. The order was given to move out and with Sam and Tye in front with Lieutenant Dixon and a Captain Ronald Humphreys, a first sergeant, two corporals and sixteen troopers headed out from the fort to who knows what trouble. Sam knew with Tye being like a magnet and Indians like steel there was going to be a coming together sooner or later and he was going to have another chance to be scalped. He smiled and shook his head.

Chapter Two

Four hours later they made camp with Tye telling them this would be the last camp with a fire and coffee so enjoy it. There was no complaining among the troops. Every one of them was a veteran of several forays into Indian country and understood that not being seen was an important point to staying alive. Besides, this was Tye Watkins leading them; a man every man on the Texas frontier knew of and respected. They watched his every move and realized he never moved without purpose and was like a big cat, graceful and quiet when he did move.

Captain Humphreys and Lieutenant Dixon came over to their fire. "Mind if we sit for a spell," Captain Humphreys asked.

"Make yourself at home Captain," Sam said and the two men squatted by the small fire with their coffee cups already full.

"I'm glad to make your acquaintance," Humphreys said to both men. "Been hearing about you for years Tye what with your goings on with the Apache. Some stories were a little hard to believe. And you Sam, Major Tinsley filled me in about your exploits as a marshal. Quite impressive."

Tye chuckled. "Some stories after being told a dozen times does get sorter stretched a mite."

Sam spoke up. "Don't you believe a thing he says about the stories, Captain. I've talked to officers, non-coms and troopers at Clark who swear every one of them is gospel. Hell, even Major Thurston, the Post Commander, has told me some so just believe what you hear."

"I think I will check on Sandy. Be back in a minute," Tye said standing up and walking away.

Sam laughed. Captain Humphreys asked. "What's so funny?"

"Tye Captain. He is the most famous man in Texas except maybe General Sam but he does not like to talk about himself and I think he saw where that conversation was headed and left before it did." He took a sip of coffee. "That man over there, as you will probably see in a day or so, is the best tracker, best fighter with fist or knives you will ever meet. He thinks like an Indian and that is why he is so successful fighting them. He knows what they are going to do before they know themselves. By the way, if he wasn't a lawman he would be known as the fastest gun alive. I'm pretty good but he is faster than me or anyone else I have come across but he doesn't want a reputation even though he has one that is growing despite he wants."

Dixon looked to see if Tye was coming back and saw he wasn't. "Can you tell me the story about his running forty miles on foot is true or not?

Sam nodded. "Spoke with a dozen men that he saved that night. The patrol was pinned down after an officer would not listen to Tye's advice. After dark the damn Apaches were throwing live rattlesnakes down on them from the cliff above where they were pinned down as well as shooting their rifles just to make sure they got no sleep. Tye snuck out and killed some of the sentries and ran to Fort Clark. Got there exhausted but got on a horse and led a company of men back to where the men were and pulled them out of the trap. Don't know for sure if it was forty miles or not but I guarantee it was at least thirty. Another thing and this is one that I've seen more than once myself. He has an uncanny ability to sniff out trouble before it happens." He chuckled. "If you hear him say 'Things are fixing to get interesting,' get your damn guns ready for trouble is fixing to come your way.

"Everything seems to be quiet," Tye said as he came back and squatted by the fire. He poured himself a cup of coffee and spoke to Captain Humphreys.

"These men with you have the look of men who has seen trouble before."

"Tinsley figured there was a good chance of trouble and didn't want any green troops on this patrol." He laughed. "I've never seen so many men volunteering for a dangerous patrol before. I think it was because of you, Tye."

"Me! Why would you think that?"

"They wanted to see if all the dang stories about you were true even if it meant maybe dying. That's quite a compliment to you."

Tye chuckled. "If you say so, but to me that's a sorry excuse to get yourself killed just wanting to see that."

Humphreys laughed. "Maybe, but I'm kind of curious myself."

Sam spoke up. "Ya'll are crazy. Hell I'm stuck with this guy, been shot twice almost scalped once, been in more shoot outs these past two and half years than the previous five years as a lawmen. Told Tye once that he was like a damn magnet because no matter where we go the Indians always show up." Everyone laughed. "So keeps your guns ready." All chuckled again.

"What's the story on First Sergeant Allen?" Tye asked.

"What do you mean?" Humphreys asked.

"He's a little long in the tooth, if you know what I mean."

Humphreys nodded and smiled. He's almost fifty from what I hear, but don't let that age fool you. He's meaner than a momma wolf with pups. He can whip any man in the fort and probably could even handle two of them at a time. Not a more respected soldier at the fort nor a better soldier."

"Figured as much," Tye said. "We have had some like that at Clark." He stared off in the distance thinking of his two close friends that was killed by the Apache; Sergeant Christian and Lieutenant Garrison. He stood up. "Think I'll get a little shut eye. "Got me a feeling things are going to get interesting real soon."

Humphreys and Lt. Dixon both looked at Sam. Sam mouthed his words so they could read his lips-*Get your guns ready* and chuckled, stood up and followed Tye to their bedrolls.

"Damn," Dixon said to no one in particular.

Humphreys said. "Check the guards and tell them to make sure they stay alert unless they want to chance their throats getting cut. Double the guards on the horses."

"Yes sir."

Lying on his ground sheet Tye whispered to Sam. "Seen some tracks of unshod ponies off to our left earlier when I was looking around. I think the Comanche know we are here. I'm going to scout around some in a couple hours and see if we can expect a surprise about daylight or not."

Chapter Three

Tye nudged Sam with the toe of his moccasin then kneeled down beside him. Sam's eyes flew open as soon as Tye nudged him. "Don't make any noise Sam," he whispered. We are going to have a hundred or more Comanche on us at first light. We need to wake the others very quietly and get them together where I can talk to them." Sam nodded and pulled his boots on after putting his hat on and started moving from one trooper to the other starting with First Sergeant Allen who helped him. Tye woke up the captain and lieutenant.

When everyone was together Tye spoke in a tone just loud enough for all to hear. "Yesterday I come across some tracks of unshod ponies to our left when I was scouting around. Later I caught a glimpse of a warrior who mistakenly got himself sky lined on the crest of a hill. Wasn't sure if was just a hunting party or not so earlier tonight I snuck out of camp to take a look around. I found a camp with at least a hundred warriors about a mile and a half in front of us. No women or children so this is a war party. I didn't want to say anything till I was sure." He waited for a moment and then continued.

"They will hit us about the first crack of daylight so to have a chance we will have to be ready for them. I understand all of you have seen some action against the Indians so you know how it will be; loud war cries, pounding of a hundred or more charging horses, and a hell of a lot of noise from the guns. Indians are hell on wheels in a fight as long as they feel they have the upper hand. They will come charging expecting us to still be in our bedrolls and it will be easy pickings for them. We will have a little surprise for them and maybe discourage them some."

"What do you want us to do Tye," Humphreys asked?

"If you noticed the lay of the land last evening when we started making camp you would have noticed the steep ridge to our right about a hundred yards away. To our left were mesquite and cactus so thick a horse would have a tough time getting thru at anything more than a walk. Behind us is a pretty steep slope that is about a couple hundred yards long and is covered by prairie dog holes. The only way they will come is head on so that is to our advantage."

"How so," a private asked?

"Several reasons son," Tye said. "First of all we will be facing northwest so the sun will not be in our faces. Second. The sun will be in their faces making it hard for them to see well enough to have any sort of accuracy. Three, surprise will be in our favor. Four, Indians don't like it when more of them are getting killed than they are killing."

"Captain, we need to move the horses behind us on that slope. Being on it and below the level we are on they won't be getting hit by stray bullets. Put a small detail to guard them. The rest of us will fort up behind our saddles in two lines. I will be in the first with my repeater and Sam will be in the second with his. At my signal, the first line will fire and then get down behind their saddles and reload while the second line is firing and then the first and so on. That way there will always be a steady fire. Have your Navy Colts beside you loaded and ready to use. I figure each line will get two shots before they will be on us. That's when you will use you revolvers and make damn sure what you are shooting at. It will be noisy, dusty and smoke so thick it will be hard to see very well, but if you keep your head we will get out of this a put a hurt on the Comanche so bad he thinks their medicine is bad and leave to fight another day."

"Do you think we really have a chance," one of the younger troopers asked?

"Hell yes we have but to do so all of you have to keep your head and not panic. I can't tell you how many troopers I have seen killed that would still be alive if they hadn't panicked. Pair up and watch each other's back and remember, if you don't do what you are supposed to do, you are going to get your partner killed as well as yourself."

"Are they any questions?"

It was quiet for a moment then a voice from one of the men in the back said. "Don't suppose they just might surrender do you Tye." Tye could have hugged that man because every man laughed even though it was a nervous laugh and he knew then they would stand their ground.

"Let's get the horses moved and form up over there in two lines about ten yards apart," Tye said. "One other thing, you men in the second line make sure you don't shoot one of your friends in the front line." Every face he could see in the darkness was smiling. He knew that would be changing as they waited.

They all settled in their places behind their saddles. Captain Humphreys was beside Tye in the front line and Lieutenant Dixon was beside Sam in the rear line. All were lost in their thoughts but had one thing in common; they knew hell was coming their way in a couple hours.

Chapter Four

Lying beside Tye Humphreys whispered a question. "What prompted you to go scouting at midnight? "

'I told you I caught a glimpse of a warrior yesterday afternoon when he sky lined himself on a small hill. Later when I was scouting around I found tracks, unshod tracks, in that direction and they were shadowing us. Wasn't sure if it was a hunting party or a war party. I went out about midnight to find out."

"You went out alone," he said shaking his head. "That was crazy."

"Capt'n, I've been fighting the Apache all my life. The Apache is the greatest fighter in the world and the best at sneaking in and killing men so If I could sneak in and around Apache camps I figured the Comanche would be easy. By the way, you need to do a little work on your men that are doing night guard. I was within three feet of one when I left and not much farther from one when I returned."

"I'll make it a point to do that-that is if we are still alive after this attack you say is coming." Tye looked at him and saw a smile on his face.

Sam and me will stay awake so pass the word to the others to get a little shuteye while they can.

"Shut eye," he said in a startled tone. "Shut eye, how in blazes do you think anyone could sleep in a situation like this.

"Then you stay awake and watch and I'll get some." He rolled over on his back and pulled his hat over his eyes. Capt'n Humphreys just stared unbelievingly at him. *That man is everything I have heard*, he thought to himself. He looked at his hands and even in the early morning chill, his palms were sweating.

A mile or so in front of the troops camp Little Wolf sat with his most trusted warriors, Running Dog, Little Bear, and Crazy Wolf. "Our scouts," he said, "have told me where the blue coats are camped. Their camp is a good one as there is only one way to attack but if we hit them just as the sun comes up with our warriors charging on their horse at full speed we should be able to surprise them and over run them." He smiled. "There will many white scalps on our lances today. There will be many more guns and bullets for our warriors. He stood up and looked over their camp. Over one hundred warriors milled about getting their war paint on themselves and their war horses. The four friends looked at each other and nodded.

"Quanah will be pleased when he hears of our great victory," Crazy Wolf said. They begin to put their own war paint on themselves and their war ponies. The Comanche were known for their great horsemanship and were called by many officers as the greatest light cavalry in the world. Each warrior had many ponies but each had one special one that was trained for war. They would not flinch at gun fire and would obey the commands of their masters by pressure from their owner's knees leaving both hands free for killing their enemies These same horses were used in the dangerous buffalo hunts.

A few minutes later with all the warriors mounted and in a circle around their leader, Little Wolf spoke. "We will walk our ponies till we are only a short distance from their camp," "When it is light enough for us to see we will charge and over run the camp killing them all." All the warriors raised their voices in a wild chant and waved their rifle or bows above their heads. They were instantly quite when Little Wolf stood on the back of his war pony. "Quiet my brothers. We want to surprise our blue coated friends." He moved his pony through the circle followed by Running dog, Little Bear, and Crazy Wolf. The others followed them.

The first gray in the eastern sky was breaking the darkness of a moonless night when Captain Humphreys whispered to Tye. "Are you sure of this Tye? I figured we would have seen or heard something by now."

"They're out there Captain. They are not the Calvary. A hundred of them can move quieter than ten soldiers. I figure they tied deer skins on their pony's hooves to help muffle the sound. When they get ready, they will take them off and charge. I'm hoping the surprise of us being ready and the two repeaters Sam and I have will be more firepower than they expected.

Fifteen minutes later a low rumbling sound in front of them could be heard and grew louder with each passing second. The ground begins to shake and the loud war cries mixed with the sound of more than four hundred hooves pounding the ground reached the soldiers.

"Don't fire till I do," Tye said loud enough to be heard over the screams and horses. "Make your shots count." A couple seconds later they could see the hoard charging at them. "HOLD!" Tye hollered. "HOLD!" At one hundred yards he hollered "FIRE" He sighted and squeezed the trigger and felt the Henry buck against his shoulder. The buck he was aiming did a back flip off his pony and tripped the pony behind him throwing the rider hard to the ground. The others fired their single shot Springfield's and he saw several more go down. He heard the second row fire as he was spraying his bullets from the Henry with a deadly accuracy. The first row fired again and he could hear the different sound of Sam's Henry from the louder Springfield's.

The charge broke and swerved to the right and then back from where they come from.

A loud cheer went up from the soldiers. Tye hollered above them and they quieted down. "It ain't over yet men. You did a good job but the surprise is over and they will reorganize and come at us again. Do we have any casualties?"

"Two dead three wounded. None of the wounded wounds are life threatening," Sergeant Allen answered.

"When will they come?" a voice came from behind him.

"When they get ready," Tye said. "They know we ain't going anywhere so they got plenty of time. Captain I know this sounds crazy but I want some men to go with me to move the dead warriors and place them off to the side."

"Why would you do that?"

"Respect, Captain. Indians respect courage but they also have an honor about them of the way they take care of their dead. If we show the dead respect and handle them with the respect one shows a fellow warrior it might just make a difference. "

"You seen this before?"

"About six or eight months ago I was at a ranch when Quanah Parker and a large group of warriors attacked. Like this time, I was fortunate enough to have the ranch ready and we caught them in a cross fire killing a lot of them. When they rode off I had them gather up the dead and gently placed them in a row. We doctored a wounded warrior and along with him, me and one of the ranch hands placed him on one of the ponies of the dead and took him and several ponies to where Quanah was. At the time we did not know it was Parker who had led the raid. Anyway, he came out to meet us by himself and we palavered for few minutes. We left and they came and got their dead and sent a beautiful decorated peace pipe to the rancher's wife who had doctored the wounded warrior. It was a sign of respect and they would never bother them again."

"You actually spoke with Quanah?"

Tye nodded. "Speaks better English than a lot of white men I know." He stood up and asked for six volunteers to help him and Sam move the dead bodies. When they were among the Indians lying on the ground Tye spoke. "I don't give a damn how you feel about the Comanche but we are going to pick them up and carry them over there and lay them in a row on the ground. I will personally kick the hell out of any one of you that does not do it gently. If you find one that is still alive you let me know. Is that perfectly clear to each one of you?" Each nodded. "Okay, let's do it but make sure they are dead before you try picking them up. Just let me or Sam know if you find one that is still alive.

When they were through twenty two dead warriors lay in a row. Three were found to be alive and Tye and Sam treated them the best they could and placed them in front of the first row of Soldiers in a sitting position and gave each a drink of water which each promptly spit out as Tye knew they would. Each one of them glared at the soldiers, hate showing in them. Not one of them showed any sign of pain but every soldier knew they were in a lot of it.

"Tough sumbitches," Sergeant Allen commented.

"That one with the stomach wound has to be hurting something fierce," another commented.

"You could hold a red hot blade to them and they would do no more than flinch," Tye said. "A warrior is taught all his life to never show two things; fear or pain to an enemy. An Indian may retreat sometimes like today for instance, but it's not because they were afraid. Great honor is bestowed on a brave and his family that dies bravely in battle and much shame would come to their family if one showed fear. A warrior has no fear of death like we do. That is why tribes like the Apache for instance that has a low number of warriors compared to the Sioux or Comanche or most other tribes are great guerilla fighters; they hit quickly, do as much damage as they can with minimum loss to their selves and retreat to live and fight another day. They live to fight their enemies and all white men are their enemies."

"I hear that Quanah Parker is the greatest white hater of them all," a private said.

"MY GOD," a private screamed and pointed. All looked in the direction he was pointing and you could hear curses, verses from the Bible and all other comments.

In front of them was maybe three hundred or more Comanche spread out in a line a hundred yards wide and many rows deep.

"We is done fur" commented one soldier.

"Heaven help us," said another.

"Get to your positions," Captain Humphreys shouted, "And as before don't fire till Tye give the word."

As they watched a warrior, obviously a chief stepped his horse forward a few steps from the others and sat there on his black war horse.

"I think that's Quanah," Tye said to Humphreys

Humphreys cleared his throat. "Is that supposed to make me comfortable or something."

Tye did not say anything, just watched the warrior as he came a few steps closer. As he watched the warrior held up both hands out away from his body and said in the universal sign language used by all tribes that he wanted to talk.

Tye stood up. "Don't a damn one of you even think about firing his rifle. That Indian, unless I'm mistaken is Quanah Parker and for some reason wants to talk so maybe we have a chance, but we won't if one of you gets trigger happy and fires his gun at him."

"What are you going to do," Humphreys asked.

Tye handed his Henry repeater and took off his belt and holster and handed them to the private next to him. "Me and Sergeant Allen are going out to meet him and have us a palaver."

"M...M...Me?" Sergeant Allen asked looking at Tye.

"Time you learned a little about Indians instead of just wanting to kill them," Tye chuckled. Allen handed his weapons to a corporal and mumbled something about this being the stupidest thing he had ever been ordered to do.

"I guess I'm ready Tye," he reluctantly said.

"You sure about this Tye?" Sam asked.

"About as sure one can be about an Indians way of thinking." He shook Sam's hand which Sam took as a bad sign. They haven't shook hands but once or twice in the years previous they had been partners.

"Let's go Sergeant," he said and both men begin walking toward the biggest hater of white men in the Comanche Nation.

Vendetta

Chapter Five

A minute later both Tye and Quanah recognized each other at the same time. Neither smiled as both understood the graveness of the situation. When they met they both sat on the ground cross legged Indian style.

"Good to see you again Watkins," Quanah said. "I figured it was you when they described the 'big' scout to me and then I was sure when I saw our dead warriors the way they were placed. You the only white man I know of that would do that."

"Good to see you Quanah," Tye answered. "I wish it was under different circumstances."

Quanah nodded." Why you here and why with the blue coats?" He looked at Allen with a glare that sent chills up and down the sergeants spine. "You know this is Comanche land."

"I know this is Comanche land. I know that Quanah is Chief of all the Quahadi band of the Comanche Nation. I know the Quahadi band is the fiercest of all Comanche bands. We are not here to trouble you or to fight you. A few days ago several men robbed a bank in the town of San Angelena near Fort Concho. Several people were killed including the nephew of the post commander at Fort Concho. I was tracking them when the Comanche attacked."

"How is it then the blue coats appeared to be ready for attack this morning?"

"I am like you Quanah Parker. I am a warrior, been fighting since I was fourteen years old. Over the years since then I seem to have a second sense that tells me when trouble was coming. Course it helped when I caught a glimpse of one of your warriors, probably a young one, that sky lined himself for a moment. I rode over to where I saw him and saw the prints of many unshod ponies. Last night, I slipped away from our camp and found the camp of the Comanche. I watched awhile and saw no women or children. I figured an attack would come at dawn."

"You picked this place to camp?" Quanah asked. Tye nodded. "You picked a good place, one that a true warrior would pick," he said looking at the surrounding terrain. You say you sneaked into our camp?"

"Not into but close enough to hear voices. At one time I was an arms length from a sentry."

Quanah smiled. "Truly you are as I have heard. An Indian in a white man's body."

Tye smiled back. "Then we are the same. You also are a white man in an Indians body," referring to Quanah having a white mother and Indian father."

"Only part white," Quanah replied back. "I have only Comanche blood in my veins." There was a moment of silence and then Quanah spoke again. "This was Little Wolfs camp you were near last night. I rode in only this morning. I did see the tracks of the white men you are following. If we can figure out how we can solve this situation here maybe you can continue to do so. The problem is there," he said pointing to the dead braves. Little Wolf is going to want revenge, want blood because of those that have died."

"We also have dead and wounded," Tye said and we did nothing to cause Little Wolf to attack."

Quanah nodded. "I will do what I can. I will get back to you." He stood up as did Tye and Allen. Quanah looked at Allen and the trooper could feel again the hate radiating from Quanah's eyes. Quanah then placed his hand on Tye's left shoulder and Tye placed his hand on the Chiefs. An instant later, Quanah turned and walked away.

"What's going to happen, Tye? Quanah seemed to want to ride away."

"He does but Indians are not like you and the other soldiers. You follow orders whether you like them or not. This is the big weakness of the Indians. They may have a chief but each warrior is his own man and makes his own decisions. We will just have to wait and see."

Arriving back to their camp they were bombarded with questions.

Captain Humphreys bellowed his order to shut up in no uncertain terms using language not always heard coming from an officer of the United States Army. It was instantly quiet. He, Tye, Sam, and Lt. Dixon walked off to the side out of earshot. Tye saw the men surround Allen.

"Tell us what happened Sergeant," everyone asked at once.

Allen, enjoying being the center of attention, took his time before speaking. "I tell you boys that was the scariest five minutes of my life. Eyeball to eyeball with the he-wolf himself."

"You mean it was Parker?"

"In the flesh," Allen said nodding. "I tell you we got the real thing in that Watkins. Parker knew who he was and has great respect for him, maybe even a little fear. We talked for a few minutes and then he left. Watkins had told him we were chasing some outlaws and had no intention of bothering the Comanche."

"Dammitt Sarge, What did that savage say about fighting us?"

"He's meeting with his sub chiefs now to decide if they kill us or not. We just wait."

Tye was talking with Humphreys. "I don't know which way it's going Captain," Tye said after explaining the conversation with Parker. "We just have to wait and hope for the best."

"What's your gut feeling," Dixon asked Tye?

Tye turned his head and spit before answering. "Can't say for sure but I don't think they will just ride away. Indians have a lot of pride, honor, duty, whatever you want to call it and those dead braves over there calling for them to revenge them."

"GAWD ALMIGHTY!!!" screamed one of troopers. All looked north where the wide-eyed trooper was pointing.

Maybe three hundred Comanche sat on their ponies a quarter mile away slowing walking their ponies toward them.

"Get to your positions men," Humphreys shouted. "Same orders as before." Each man including Tye and Sam knew it was over for them if the Comanche attacked. There was too many of them for their little troop to turn back and they would be overrun with the first attack.

Men thought of their wives and children; some of girlfriends and those with no one thought of never having another cold one with their buddies at the saloon. Tye was no different. Pictures of Rebecca and the kids flashed across his mind and his eyes watered at the thought. The thoughts were erased when Quanah approached the troop by himself.

"Hold your fire," Captain Humphreys ordered. He and Tye stood up when Quanah was within talking distance.

"We're fixing to get our answer Captain," Tye said in a low voice.

Vendetta

Chapter Six

Tye and Humphreys approached Quanah as Quanah slide off his pony's back. The officer was appraising the warrior and was surprised from the man's fierce reputation he wasn't bigger than he was. Quanah appeared to about five nine give an inch or so and built on rather the slim line, but as he watched the man approach he could see the muscles and strength in that build. It was apparent if one looked close that he was part white but you could also tell this was one tough, mean Comanche.

"Quanah," Tye said speaking first. "This is Captain Humphreys from Fort Concho." Humphreys offered his hand but it was ignored as Quanah looked at Tye.

"I have spoken with the others and explained why you were here. It fell mostly on deaf ears." Tye saw Humphreys stiffen.

"The want blood, want revenge for those lying yonder," he said nodding toward the bodies of the warriors. "I told them enough has died this day no need for many more to die. This is what they want Watkins. All have heard of you; Watkins the great Indian killer, the man who cannot be killed; the white man who is more warrior than any other white man."

Tye knew what was coming before Quanah even said it, a test of combat, a test of who knew what but it wasn't going to be nice.

"They want you or at least Little Wolf does. He is a great warrior Watkins, a man whose name is known among the Comanche as you are among the whites and the Apache. Little Wolf says you and him will fight with knives in the Comanche way. If he wins all soldiers die. If you win soldiers will live and can continue their quest for the other white men. Do you agree?"

Humphreys looked at Tye. "You don't have to do this Tye. We will fight"

"No need Captain. If I don't they will kill all of us" He looked at Quanah and nodded. "When?"

"In a short time. He has to prepare himself." He leaped on is pony and rode back to the others.

Tye and Humphreys walked back to where Sam, Dixon and the others were waiting.

"What did Quanah say Captain?" Lieutenant Dixon asked. All the others were anxiously waiting for the answer also.

Humphreys looked all in the eye. "They want blood, all our blood." He could see the look of fear, anguish, and the hope of maybe living disappear in their face. "We have one chance to live," he said and saw their heads rise up and looked him. "They will settle for one life."

"What does that mean Captain?" a trooper asked.

"They will settle for Tye. They want, or should I say the leader of the ones who attacked us wants a hand to hand fight with knives with Tye. If he wins we all will die but if Tye wins, we can continue unmolested our hunt for the outlaws."

"You gonna do this?" Sam asked.

Tye smiled and nodded. "Don't look like I have much of a choice." He took off his belt and holster and gave it to Sam. He took off his hat. He took the Bowie from the sheath in his right moccasin boot. Walking over to where his saddle lay he took a flat rock out of one of his saddle bags and at down on the saddle and began sharpening the blade.

Sergeant Allen came over in a few minutes and sat on the saddle next to him as did San and Captain Humphreys on saddles. "Just wanted to let you know Tye how much all of us appreciate what you are trying to do for us. If you can win this fight and we live we'll be indebted to you the rest of our lives and if you don't...well we appreciate it anyway and we will die a soldier's death. He stuck out his hand which Tye took. "Good Luck and may all the Saints be with you."

Tye took out a shirt from the other saddle bag and cut it into strips and then took out a flask that he carried for this purpose. It was full of whiskey, not for drinking but for wounds to keep infection down. He handed the flask and strips to Allen. I'm going to be cut regardless of whether I win or not so have these handy in case I do win."

"Here they come," a trooper said. Tye stood up and looked. He then kneeled and bowed his head and prayed. When the others saw almost all of them kneeled and prayed in their own way a prayer for deliverance, a prayer for Tye, a prayer for forgiveness and lastly, a prayer for their death to be quick if they were to die.

Tye stood up and pulled his deer skin shirt over his head. As usual Sam saw the looks of awe in the faces of the troopers not only of the muscular build but of all the scars that covered his upper torso. Lieutenant Dixon stared with his mouth open in disbelief.

"How in God's name are you alive, Tye?" He asked.

"I can answer that Lieutenant," Sam said. "The surgeon at Fort Clark says he can never die because he has no vital organs, no heart, no lungs, nothing but muscle and bone." Dixon looked at Sam and saw he was laughing. Some of the men smiled but it was a nervous type smile. Sam looked at Tye. "Good luck pard," and shook Tye's hand.

"In Comanche stlye knife fighting even the winner is going to be cut so be ready with that whiskey and bandages. You might find some rawhide to use as a tourniquet if needed also."

Tye turned and nodded to the men and turned back and started a slow walk to where the Comanche waited for what he knew was going to be a painful fight to the death.

Chapter Seven

Little Wolf dropped to his knees and began to chant. He picked up a handful of dirt and holding it up opened his hand and let the wind take the dirt away. He chanted, or sang for a full minute and then picked up more dirt and let it fall from his hand. He then stood up and faced Tye. A warrior came from the ranks and using a piece of buffalo hide, tied the two men's left arms together from the wrist to the elbow. Quanah came forward and spoke in the Comanche language to his warriors. He then turned to the troops and in almost perfect English, repeated what he had said. "If Little Wolf wins you will all die. If Watkins wins you will be allowed to pursue the men you are after but will return to the fort you come from when it is done."

He turned to the two gladiators and looked up at the blue sky and held his arms above his head, chanted some words in Comanche. He then had the men square off and he held their left hand in his. Tye' Bowie was placed in his right hand and Little Wolf's in his right hand. Quanah held their hands and then released them and jumped back quickly. This was the signal to start.

Only the cat like quickness of Tye save him from a nasty wound as he sucked his stomach in and stepped back as far as he could as Little Wolf swept his blade at his stomach the instant Quanah let go of their hands.

Tye countered with a stab at his opponent's thigh and saw his blade strike flesh. The razor sharp edge cut deep in the side of Little Wolfs thigh and was bleeding profusely. Tye saw the look of surprise in his opponent's eyes. Shouts came from the soldiers when they saw the blood but was instantly quiet as they saw the Comanche's blade slice deep in Tye's left upper arm and blood pouring forth. Tye paid no attention to the the pain and struck with his blade deep into Little Wolf's left shoulder and ripped it out the side. The warriors left arm was useless now and he was bleeding badly from two wounds now. They circled and feinted and blocked each thrust of their opponent.

Tye was feeling a little light headed as he knew the Comanche had to be. *I need to end this now*, he thought to himself. Bracing himself he jerked the warrior toward him and falling to the ground on his back himself threw the man over him. Little Wolf hit the ground on his back hard stunning him for just a second and that was all the time Tye needed. He was immediately astride the man's chest and placed the blade of his Bowie on the throat of Little Wolf. The warrior had lost his knife when he hit the ground. He looked at Quanah and the chief nodded his understanding Tye was the winner.

Tye stood up, chest heaving and gulping in air. He looked at Quanah again and thought he saw a slight smile. He turned and walked toward the soldiers who were yelling and celebrating their escape from death.

Sam yelled, "TYE, LOOK OUT!!

Without wondering why Tye took his partners words to heart and dodged to his right just as a knife grazed his shoulder and suck in one of the troopers saddles in front of him. He twisted around just in time to see Quanah slash Little Wolf's throat with his butcher knife.

Quanah looked at Tye and saw he was okay and nodded. He yelled something in Comanche and the hoard mounted their ponies and rode off. The soldiers mobbed Tye at once congratulating him, thanking God and already making up more stories about the scout turned marshal.

Tye stepped away and said, "Thanks men but if I don't stop this bleeding I ain't going to be around to save your sorry butts again." He laughed along with all the rest.

Sam came over with the bandages and whiskey. Captain Humphreys looked at the wound and told Sergeant Allen to get the needle and thread from his saddle bag. Tye looked at him questionably. "It's not going to stop bleeding unless it's sewed up Tye." Tye looked at the wound and nodded.

Sam would pour a little whiskey on it, Tye would cuss, and Humphreys would take another stitch-twelve in all before the bleeding stopped.

"Good job 'Doc'," Tye said smiling to Humphreys. "We better get mounted and move on Captain. Indians are notional critters and some who don't fear Quanah may come back and pay us a visit. Sam and me will make a couple travois and you can send a couple men back to the fort with the wounded and the dead can be wrapped and tied to their mounts."

"Are you up to it, Tye?" Humphreys asked as Tye picked up his saddle and walked toward Sandy. Humphreys looked at Sam. Sam just shrugged and picked up his saddle.

Damn man is unbelievable, Humphreys thought to himself. *Just had a life or death fight, half bled to death and here he is leading us on and acting like it was no big deal.*

An hour later Tye reined Sandy to a halt. Humphreys raised his arm and the patrol came to a halt.

In front of them came a Comanche with his right arm up, palm out in the peace sign. Tye rode out t meet him keeping an eye all around for a trap. He pulled up in front of the warrior and also gave the peace sign.

"Quanah told me to show you where the men you seek are," he said in broken English.

Tye nodded. "Quanah is a great Chief and his people are honorable."

"Little Wolf had no honor."

Tye nodded. "What name do you go by." Tye asked.

Howling Coyote," the brave said sitting straight as an arrow and chest out proud as a peacock.

Tye nodded. "How far to these men?"

Howling Coyote looked over his shoulder. "Two moons."

"You ride beside me?" Tye asked.

Howling Coyote nodded. Tye turned in the saddle and motioned the troop to come on.

He explained the situation to Humphreys and added that since Howling Coyote knows just about where they are we can make good time not having to follow tracks. Humphreys asked if he could be trusted.

"Did you see what Quanah did to Little Wolf Captain?" The captain nodded. "Indians, all Indians, have one thing in common-they don't lie and their honor is unbelievable. Little Wolf back there lost his temper and you saw what it got him. Yes, Captain, he can be trusted, and I expect you and your men treat him as the warrior he is- with respect. "

Humphreys nodded and turned to Sergeant Allen. You heard Tye. Pass the word."

"Yes Sir," Allen said saluting.

Tye looked at Howling Coyote and smiled. "Lead the way."

Chapter Eight

They made camp just before dusk. Tye and Howling Coyote went ahead to scout saying they would be back about dark. Squatting around their fires most of the discussions concerned the earlier event of Tye saving each of their butts.

Captain Humphreys, Lieutenant Dixon, Sam, and Corporal Dixon were around one fire and their conversation was no different from the others.

"I swear if I live to be a hundred I'll never see another thing like that," Dixon said. "That man is more man than any three men I have ever known. Hell, Davy Crockett has nothing on him," he chuckled.

"I've seen that man do things that are just damn unbelievable the last three years. In my years as a lawman I've seen a lot of fast draws, Hitchcock, Masterton, Stoudiemire, John Wesley Hardin, and a few more but Tye could beat all of them. I seen him try to talk a youngster out of drawing on him awhile back—tried everything he could think of, but the young man went for his gun." He hesitated for a few seconds.

"Dammit man," Dixon said. "What happened?"

"What he did showed just what a man he is. He fired his gun before the youngster had even cleared leather. He could have killed him but he shot him in the right shoulder. He then put his arm around him and talked to him till the doc got there. The youngster was the son of a prominent rancher and when his father got there and found out exactly what happened he walked over with tears in his eyes and thanked Tye for not killing his son. Even the son came back over to him before he left and although hurting something bad, shook Tye's hand saying he had learned a lesson and was going to be content to be just a cow puncher. I told Tye he was crazy to have done that, just wounding the boy instead of killing him. If he had missed he would have been dead. His answer, 'he was just a kid Sam. No way was I going to kill him, just try and teach him a lesson.' I just shook my head at him knowing that's the man he is and no one or anything is going to change him. But I tell you, I've watched that man practice for hours around our campfires and you have never, I mean never seen anything as quick, not even a rattlesnake strike."

"What about all the stories about him and the Apaches," Humphreys asked.

He's been fighting and killing them just about his whole life. Killed his first one when he was fourteen with a knife. His pa was a mountain man, a quite famous one I might add, and since Tye was old enough to walk taught him all the skills he could in knife and tomahawk fighting, tracking and reading sign, fist fighting and wrestling.

"Watkins...Watkins," Corporal Allen said then snapped his fingers. "Ben Watkins! Was Ben his father?"

"Yep," Sam said. "He's right up there with Bridger and all the other trappers that made a name for themselves back in the twenties and thirties in the Rockies. Matter of fact, Shakespeare McDovitt trapped with his father and Jim Bridger and now lives with Tye and his wife back at Fort Clark. I've been privileged to listen to that old man talk about those days and what a man Ben Watkins was. Buff, that's what Shakespeare likes to be called, is way over seventy now but gets around like a man thirty years younger and is sharp as a tack. He has led several patrols himself and has the respect of every man on the fort just like Tye does."

"Listening to those stories about life in the Rockies makes a man wonder if he could have done it if he had lived back then. Living outside in the cold of winter when it would be twenty to thirty below zero at times and snow up to man's ass for six or more months of the year." He laughed and said. "I heard him tell Rebecca one time that they would go months without a good hot bath."

Lieutenant Dixon spoke up. "Well I'll tell you this when he took his shirt off I've never seen more muscles on a man in my life and all those scars. Damn man, how is he alive?"

Sam laughed. "Like I said, the post surgeon at Clark says he has no vital organs and can't die." He chuckled, "Tye says every damn one of them has a story too." He thought for a minute and then added. "I think at last count its eight knife scars, three arrows, six bullet, and one tomahawk wound. All that's left is a spear wound and he says he don't want no part of a spear," he added laughing.

"Well, he's the most remarkable man I have ever met," Captain Humphreys muttered shaking his head. "I'm damn glad he was with us when all this came about or every dang one of us would be lying out there in the dirt."

"Riders coming in," one of the night guards hollered.

Tye and the Comanche warrior Howling Coyote rode into the camp dismounted and walked to the supply wagon. Tye grabbed a tin cup for himself and one for Howling Coyote. Knowing Indians for the most part like coffee but with lots of sugar he grabbed a handful from the supply wagon and poured it into the warrior's cup. The cup will be hot he whispered to the Comanche not wanting him to be the center of jokes when he burned his lips.

They walked to the fire where Sam and the officers were and picking up the coffee pot filled both cups with coffee and squatted by the fire with everyone else.

"What did you find," Captain Humphreys asked.

Tye took a sip and replied. "They are holding up during the day and traveling by night. We found the camp they used yesterday."

"So we are only a day behind?"

Tye nodded. "Looks that way Captain. They don't appear to be in a hurry. They are smart enough to hole up during the day though."

'What do you suggest we do then?"

Sam was impressed with this officer. He saw him a couple times during the fight with the Comanche and he handled himself well. He showed good sense now in asking for Tye's opinion which he knew most young officers would not do."

"I suggest we get about four or five hours rest then we get an early start about three hours before daylight and then travel during the day resting periodically while they are holed up. With luck I think we can catch up tomorrow night or early the next day."

"Sergeant Allen."

"Yes sir."

"Pass the word that each man will be ready to ride about three hours before daylight so they need to get some sleep now. Be sure the guard schedule is set before you retire."

Sergeant saluted the captain. "Yes sir. Will do Sir." He turned sharply and walked to the other two fires.

Several miles ahead Jesse lambert and his men saddling their mounts and preparing to move out like they had done the previous nights. He didn't think the

Comanche were prone to move around the country a lot at night. He figured the warriors had rather be beating drums, doing their crazy war dances or making babies than riding on this lonely damn prairie at night. He had been right so far as they had seen not nary an Indian.

"How much farther till we get out of Injun territory Jesse," Kip, his most trusted man asked?

"Not sure Kip," he answered. "Never been here before but according to the map if I'm reading it right, no more than two more days of travel and then we will head east toward the Oklahoma Badlands."

"Boys are sorter anxious to get some cash in their pockets and were wondering when you were planning to split the money with them."

Jesse exploded. "They will get their damn money when I say and not before! If any of them sumbitches don't like it they can come and try to take it."

Kip threw up his hands. "Whoa boss. Settle down. They were just wondering is all." Kip knew that Jesse was a man you had better walk on egg shells around. He had been in gangs before and seen his share of bad men, but none held a candle to Jesse. Kip thought as he mounted his horse, *this man has the most explosive temper he had ever seen, able to fly off the handle at the smallest thing. Those killings back in San Angelina had been unnecessary. This is the third job I have been on with him and there was unnecessary killing in every one of them. That young man he shot down on the board walk was no threat. I saw him clearly and I don't think he was even armed. Now, because of the direction we left town in we are in the middle of damn Comanche country and have had no coffee for three or four days because Jesse didn't want no smoke. Cowboys, outlaws, or any man going a full day without coffee can get downright ornery and if he goes two or three days things can really get tense. Jesse may not realize it yet but he's riding a damn powder keg.*

As they rode Kip continued to think about things. *Things are changing out here. Use to be the people figured a robbery was done by a out of work cowboy and if no one was hurt they sorter overlooked it since they figured the banks were robbing them too on loans, deeds, foreclosures and so forth. They would form a posse and chase the outlaws but their heart wasn't in it and would give up pretty quick. It was a hell of lot different when some of their citizens were killed in the process of the robbery. The telegraph spreading news all over the country, town sheriffs and marshals starting to work together would continue to increase the risk of getting caught and hung. I think if I get away this time I'm done and look for something else. I got some money saved might start up a saloon somewhere with some pretty girls for entertainment. He smiled at that thought.*

Chapter Nine

Tye and Howling Coyote stood where the outlaws had camped.

"I make it out that we are three to four hours behind them," Tye said after looking around.

Howling Coyote nodded in agreement pretty amazed this white man could read sign this well. "No more than half day, maybe less."

The troops sat on their mounts just away from the camp while Tye and the Comanche looked around. Tye walked over to Captain Humphreys.

"We are at the most I think four hours behind this bunch. I suggest we take a short break and give the horses a blow then get after them. I think we can catch them camped before they take off again at dark.

Humphreys turned to Lt. Dixon and gave the order for a short break. Dixon turned to Sgt. Allen and told him to give the order to the men. Tye smiled at the scene. *It would be a lot easier if Capt. Humphreys just turned in the saddle and gave the order but that ain't the army way.* Tye smiled. *Army protocol is so much crap.*

"Exactly how many of them are they," Capt. Humphreys asked while chewing a cold biscuit and a piece of bacon.

"From the looks of the tracks where the horses were picketed I figure six. Looking around the camp at the boot tracks I figure one of them is a Mexican."

Humphreys looked at Tye. "How do you figure that?"

While they were squatting and talking one of the men has those Mexican spurs with the big rowels that dug into the ground. One of them limps when he walks; maybe caught a stray bullet or may just be crippled but he is a big man."

"That would be Jesse," Sam said.

Humphreys shook his head and smiled. "I guess you can tell us what they were eating too."

"Yep," Tye answered. "Same as us hard tack and biscuits." Humphreys and Dixon looked at the man and both knew he was telling the truth.

Lt. Dixon asked Tye a question. "Since we have a few minutes Tye I would like to know something if you don't mind." Tye looked at him and nodded. "I've read a lot of books like most of the men here about the lives that the mountain man lived. Are those dime novels pretty accurate are they stretching thins a mite?" Some of the men when hearing this moved a little closer so they could hear what Tye said.

Tye stopped chewing, swallowed and took a sip of water to wash things down. "I've never read many of them but saw some that my pa had about him. Pa said they were pretty accurate about the things that happened but took a lot of liberties with the truth. He said it helped sell them," he added chuckling.

He spoke again. "Pa told me a lot of things about the struggles a trapper had in the Rockies back then which I was a little skeptical of some of them. I wanted to believe him but I just could not fathom how anyone could survive some of the things he talked about. About five years ago a man came to Fort Clark looking for me. He was dressed in buckskins and was old. He gave me a letter that my pa had written to him years earlier. This old man was my fathers and Bridger's partner back in those 'shining times' as they were called by the trappers. He still lives with my wife and me and he has told me stories that were exactly how pa told me."

Tye took a swallow of water. "Let me describe a winter in the mountains to you like pa and Buff told me. Buff is the name Bridger gave Shakespeare McDovitt, the man living with me and Rebecca. The snow started in October, sometimes in September and you were ass deep for months. Sometimes the snow was more than twenty feet deep and the temperature was twenty to thirty below. Blizzards were common and you were in real trouble if you got caught away from shelter when the wind was thirty to fifty miles per hour and the temperature below zero." He laughed and said. "Pa said Jim Bridger told some greenhorns one time that it was so cold up in those mountains that if you said something to your partner you had to wait till spring for the words to thaw out so you knew what he said." Everyone laughed. "No one knows how many men came to those mountains to trap over the years so no one knows how many didn't survive. Buff said they had a rendezvous ever year where all the trappers met for two weeks and sold their pelts to the buyers who came there. Every year they were several that did not show up that he knew. He estimated that maybe as high as sixty percent died or was killed. Between the Blackfoot, the grizzly, injuries, and the bitter winters a lot did not make it. A lot almost starved or froze their first year and just went back to civilization."

Tye stood up. "I told Captain Humphreys while ago that we were not far behind the men we are chasing. They are holed up now waiting on dark to move again. If we push it I think we can surprise them before dark if we can find their camp." Someone in the background said "then let's go the sumbitches and get back to Fort Concho and some cold beer." Everyone laughed and went to their mounts and in a few minutes they were on their way.

Two hours before sundown the troopers were thinking they would spend another night without finding the bandits when they saw Tye and Howling Coyote coming toward them. The troop halted and Capt. Humphreys and Lt. Dixon along with Sam rode out to meet them.

Tye reined in and waited on them. Humphreys asked, "Did you find the camp?"

"Yes sir," Tye said. "They are about a mile farther along the trail and they are sleeping with only one man watching that I could see."

"How many?"

"Six, like I told you before," Tye answered smiling.

"Smart ass," Humphreys said laughing. "You have a plan?"

"He always has a plan," Sam chuckled.

"They are camped in a draw so with the exception of the man on guard everyone else is below the level of the ground which will give them a pretty good defensive position unless we can eliminate the guard and then surprise them.

"I suppose you have a plan that will eliminate the guard in broad daylight?"

"We will let Howling Coyote do that for us, Captain. Indians have been sneaking up on the white man for years. It's a game to them. If he can't get close enough to knife him he will use his bow and hit the man with an arrow. No noise, dead sentry."

"Sergeant Allen get the men ready to move out and check their weapons."

"Yes sir, Captain." Allen saluted and turned to the men.

"You heard the captain. Check your weapons and be ready to move out in five minutes."

Five minutes later the patrol was on the move toward the showdown with Jesse and his gang. Tye figured they would fight no matter what since they knew a noose was waiting for them back at San Angelina. It was going to get bloody.

Chapter Ten

A few minutes later Tye halted the patrol. "We're close Captain. We need absolute silence till the fight begins."

"When they see the Calvary do you really think they will fight," Humphreys asked?

"What would you do Captain if you knew if you gave up you would be facing a hanging? No man wants to hang. This is a tough outfit and they will go down fighting. Live by the bullet and die by the bullet. That's been my experience with these types of men since I started chasing them instead of Apaches."

Humphreys nodded. "I think we need to have half of the men circle and come in from the other direction and box them in."

Tye nodded his agreement. "That's exactly what I was going to suggest. I will take seven of the men and do that. Give me twenty minutes to get in position. Watch Howling Coyote and when he kills the guard attack quickly." He told the Comanche warrior about the guard and the attack would come when he killed him. Tye figured it would take fifteen or twenty minutes for the warrior to do it.

Lt. Dixon and six men were ready to ride by the time Tye was through talking with the Comanche. Sam would go with Captain Humphreys. Tye and the men trotted their mounts off to the left and would circle about a half mile west of the camp and then close in from the north.

Humphreys watched Howling Coyote as he approached the guard. Sometimes he was moving in a crouch, sometimes crawling on all fours and as he got closer, on his belly. Humphreys was dumbfounded. He had heard of the ability of the Comanche to disappear, blend in with the terrain and do it without a sound, but watching it happen before his eyes was shocking. Looking at the guard he could see nothing but open ground in front of him with nothing but a few cactus and patches of sagebrush for the Indian to hide behind. He looked back at the Comanche who was about forty yards away behind a large clump of cactus that was four or so feet high. He watched as the warrior got to his knees and took the bow from his back and notched a arrow.

Suddenly the guard stood up and walked to the Warriors right. This was the opportunity Howling Coyote was waiting for as the man had his back to him. Standing up he pulled the arrow to his ear, aimed and released it. The deadly shaft sped through the air making no noise. The point hit the man between the shoulder blades and the tip protruded six inches out his chest. The man dropped his rifle and stood there a couple seconds looking down at the shaft and wondered what happened. He dropped to his knees, tried to scream as the pain hit him but only a low gurgling sound came from his throat as blood spewed from his lips. Two seconds later he fell face forward to the dirt and died.

"Follow me men," Humphreys shouted as he kicked his mount into a gallop.

Sam was right behind him and thinking this officer was all right. Sam could see the blue clad shirts of the men with Tye coming in from the other direction and then all hell broke loose. Bullets were flying in their direction and bullets from the soldiers were cutting the air back at the bandits. Horses were going down and bullets were finding the soldiers in an alarming number.

Tye and his troops were busy as well but their bullets were finding their marks as the outlaws position on his side was not as protected as well as the side Sam was charging from. A bullet cut a gash across his upper left arm and his bullet hit the man who fired at him square in the chest knocking him backwards and falling face first in the sand of the gulley. Lt. Dixon riding beside him was knocked of his horse and hit the ground hard. Tye saw another trooper swept off his mount. They were less than thirty yards from the bandit's position when Tye gave the signal to rein in, dismount and continue fighting on foot.

Sam never felt the slug that took him off his mount and under the hooves under of the horse just behind him. Captain Humphreys was still in front of his troops and proving to all his expertise firing from a running horse with his Navy Colt.

Tye saw one man grab a mount and left the draw running all out to the west but he was too busy to think that much about it. He was in the draw and face to face with the remaining bandits. He picked up a Henry one of the bandits dropped and firing from the waist knocked one of the men down and pulling the trigger again the pin fell on an empty chamber. He never slowed and reversing the rifle and holding it by the barrel swung it like a war club catching one man in the side of the head splitting the butt of the rifle as well as the outlaws skull spraying blood and brain matter in the faces of the two men left. They immediately threw up their arms surrendering. The remaining troops were now in the gulley and disarmed the two and throwing them to the ground and tying their hands behind their backs.

Tye looked around and didn't see Sam. "Where's Sam Captain?"

"I saw him go down Tye but don't know how bad he was hit."

Tye was out of the draw in a bound and rushed where he saw Sam lying in the dirt. "No!" he hollered when he saw Sam's unmoving crumpled body lying in the dirt. He rushed over, sat down and picked up Sam's head and held it against his chest. "No God...please God...Not Sam...please, please." He looked at Sam and saw his friend's eyes open.

"Tye," he gasped. "M...my mom and pa," struggling desperately to speak. "T...tell them I l..love t... ." Te took a last gasp and died.

Tye sat there holding his friend against his chest and rocking back and forth, tears running down his face. "I will my friend. I promise you I will.

Humphreys and the other soldiers stayed away from Tye and his friend but had Sergeant Allen check on the troopers that were down including Lt. Dixon.

A few minutes later Tye gathered himself and lying Sam gently to the ground walked over to the troops. He roughly jerked one of the bandits up from the ground and got in his face growled, "Which one of you bastards is Jesse?"

The man was too slow answering and Tye slapped him hard across the face with the back of his hand, the sound loud in the evening stillness. "You have one more chance you son-of-a-bitch!"

The man spit tobacco on Tye's boots. Tye spun the big man around and using his Bowie cut the ropes from his hands. "You're going to talk to me or I am going to beat you death."

The man, feeling confident that he could whip this man, swung a right fist at Tye's head. Tye ducked and slammed a right of his own hard to the man's stomach striking him just above the navel. Gasping the man stepped back which proved to be a mistake. Tye hit him flush on the nose with a tremendous right and followed that with a left uppercut to the chin which lifted the man off his feet and he landed on his back. Tye, never feeling fury like this stepped up to the man and jerked him to his feet.

"Come on big man; let's see how tough you are. You sure as hell ain't showed me much yet." Captain Humphreys put his hand on Tye's shoulder.

"Let it be Tye." He said then shuddered when Tye looked at him. Never, in all his life had he seen the look that was in Tye's eyes. He stepped back startled.

"I'll let it be Captain when this bastard tells me what I need to know." He ducked when the outlaw took a half hearted swing at his head and then hit the man on the left cheek with a hard right that split the man's cheek open from just below his left eye down almost to the corner of his mouth.

The man went to his knees and Tye grabbed him by the collar and was fixing to hit him again when the man gasped, "Okay...okay. Tye turned him loose and the man sat down hard.

"The sorry piece of horse-shit ran out on us. Left us to fight. If I ever see him again I swear I'll kill him."

Tye reached down and jerked him to his feet. The man threw both hands in front of his face. "I aint going to hit you again but you will never get the chance to kill Jesse yourself."

"W...why?"

"Because I'm going to kill the bastard myself and it's not going to be a quick one." He turned to Captain Humphreys and with the fury that was in him somewhat spent he said. "Can you and I talk?"

"Sure," Humphreys said and walked off a ways followed by Tye.

"I guess I need to apologize for what just happened but with Sa...".

He was cut short by Humphreys. "No need Tye. I understand and so do the men."

"I'm going to track Jesse down Captain and I'm not bringing him back. I'm going to kill him Apache style because that is what he deserves." He took the badge off his shirt and handed it over to the officer. When you get back to Fort Concho wire the U.S. Marshals office and tell them I have resigned. Wire Major Thurston at Fort Clark and tell him to tell my wife about Sam and that I am going after the man responsible. Also, If possible hold the hanging till I get back so I can watch those two get what they deserve."

Humphreys nodded. "You don't have to turn in your badge you know."

"Yes I do because I do not want that badge and what it stands far to keep me from doing what I am going to do. I've watched you for days now, Captain. I watched you before the attack by the Comanche and I watched you during the fight off and on. From what I saw today, you leading your men from the front in that charge you have a lot of nerve and you will be a great officer and probably be a worthless damn general one day," he chuckled.

"Heaven forbid," Humphreys said laughing. For the first time he saw the blood on Tye upper arm. "Before you leave let's look at that arm."

"I have a little drinking whiskey left that will keep it from getting infected. Look at your wounded. I have about a hour of daylight left so I'm getting on Jesse's trail. Take care of Sam for me and see that he receives the burial he deserves. What casualties did you have?"

"Four dead and four wounded but none of the wounded is serious. I will make sure Sam is taken care of properly." He shook Tye's hand. "You catch Jesse and do what you have to do and then come by Fort Concho on your way back to Fort Clark.

Tye nodded and walked over to the men and shook each man's hand. He dropped to one knee beside the wounded Lt. Dixon. "You are going to be alright Lieutenant. I'll see you when I'm done doing what I have to do." He shook the young officer's hand and walked to

Sandy, mounted and rode off leaving the soldiers watching. Each one of the men felt they had been privileged to have had the opportunity to know the man, to ride and fight with the man, the man who was a legend in Texas. Each of them would probably add to the legend.

Vendetta

Gary McMillan

Tye Watkins

in

Vendetta

Introduction

Tye is on the trail of the outlaw Jesse Lambert the man responsible for Sam, his partner and friends death. He has turned his badge in because he did not want to be held back by the restrictions he would have as a marshal preventing him from doing what he had to do. It was to be a long and dangerous trail as they were in Comanche territory. Quanah Parker had told him he would be safe until his quest was completed but Quanah's band was not the only band of Comanche in this part of Texas. There was also a few Cheyenne and Kiowa that had not surrendered to the army as of yet though most were already on reservations. He was going to need all of his survival skills to survive this quest he had set out on.

Chapter One

Tye squatted by his small fire that was surrounded by rocks to keep prying eyes from seeing the flames. He was in Indian country so it was imperative to remain out of sight as much as possible. He had chosen the camp carefully with it being located in a six foot deep old Buffalo wallow. This was the second night he had been on the trail of Jesse Lambert who he felt was responsible for the death of his good friend and partner's death.

He was a little despondent tonight. It was only the second night in three years he had been on the trail without Sam being around to talk to. Last night was the first but he had been so tired after the fight with the outlaw he fell right to sleep. Tonight was different. He was fairly rested and was thinking about his friend. *Sam was funny, always quipping about this or that, complaining about Tye's being like a magnet always attracting Indians and he was going to get killed and scalped by this magnetism. Now he was dead, not by an Indian arrow or bullet but by an outlaw's bullet; by a outlaw that came from his friends past. He had told me he and Jesse were destined to meet again and one would die because that was what Jesse promised him when Sam had caught him and sent him to prison. His dedication to enforcing the law was inspiring to me.* He looked up at the night sky that was decorated by a million stars on this moonless night. "Lord, you received a good man yesterday in Sam Jenkins. You take good care of my friend you hear. Take good care of him." Tye dropped his chin to his chest and wept uncontrollably.

Daylight found him on the trail again. He could see how a man that was not wise to the trail could get lost in this part of Texas. No landmarks to go by and only the sun to tell you what general direction one was traveling. He had heard stories about the wagon train captains always placing a wagon tongue at night camp in the direction they were traveling to point the way the next day. It was endless miles of grass and flat land with only an occasional small hill to break the horizon. It wasn't too difficult to read Jesse's tracks because of the matted grass his horse's hooves left. This told him he was staying close because the grass would right itself in a matter of hours. He thought there would be a quarter moon tonight since last night he thought was the last of the moonless nights. If so, if there were no clouds he might just have enough light to follow the tracks and close the gap between him and Jesse even more.

It was about noon when he pulled Sandy up sharply. He dismounted and studied the tracks of several horses and he was sure they were tracks of Indian ponies since he was positive no patrols were out here. He also realized they were probably no more than an hour old. He stood up and walked over to Sandy and took one of his canteens and taking off his hat poured a little water from the canteen in it. Offering it to Sandy the big horse sucked up the water while Tye scratched him between the ears and looking in the direction the tracks were going. Indians, ever alert while traveling had seen Jesse's tracks and were now following them.

This is going to make my tracking a lot easier, he thought, *but at the same time a hell of lot more dangerous. Looks to me there are at least five Indians following Jesse and five is a lot for a man alone to contend with.* He took a piece of hardtack from his saddle bags that Captain Humphreys had given him and munched on it washing it down with a little of his precious water.

From what I learned from Humphreys the only water I was going to find were two small streams, the Colorado and then farther west the Pecos so Sandy and me are going to have to stretch what little we have with him getting the most since I may need him fresh and ready to run at any moment. He smiled at a thought that crossed his mind. *This ain't going to be the first time I have gotten a little thirsty.* He stepped into the saddle, checked his Colt to make sure it was fully loaded and then did the same with his Henry rifle. He reached behind his back checking his belt loops for shells. Almost all held a bullet and with the box of forty-five's for his Colt and two boxes of 44 caliber for the Henry in the saddle bags he felt he had enough fire power. He studied the land in front of him and then nudged Sandy forward.

Being early May the weather was a little warm but not hot like it would be in three or four weeks. He was mesmerized by the grass moving back and forth with the light breeze that was blowing in his face. *Looks like waves in a lake,* he thought watching the foot high grass moving with the wind.

He reined in Sandy and looked at the tracks. The horses were galloping now. *They must feel like they are really close to Jesse now or maybe even spotted him,* he thought. At that instant the breeze in his face carried the sound of gun shots. He kicked Sandy into a gallop. A minute later the gunfire was much louder. He was getting close, real close. He slowed Sandy to a walk and had his Henry out with its sixteen rounds of forty-fours in the sleeve. He worked the lever and chambered a round.

Five minutes later he approached a small hill that rose maybe thirty feet in height above the relative flat terrain. The gunshots seem to be just on the other side. He dismounted and picketed Sandy and started up the small hill. Just before he reached the top he took off his hat and traveled the last few feet on his belly. Peering over the hill he saw Jesse about sixty or so yards away in a buffalo wallow which he was fortunate to find. He counted six warriors spread out below him and one that was obviously dead. They were on their bellies slowly moving through the grass toward their intended victim.

Tye watched for a moment amazed as he was always was at how an Indian could move without much cover so silently, so unseen. His advantage was he was looking down on them and could see them plainly but he was sure Jesse could not see death creeping closer and closer.

Tye took a deep breath and aimed the Henry at the closest warriors back and squeezing the trigger. The butt nudged his shoulder and the bullet sped toward its target. The warrior's body jerked once when the heavy shell struck and then never moved again. Tye had already swung the Henry toward another target and squeezed another shot off. The second warrior had turned his body to look behind him to see where the shot had come from and the bullet hit him in the ribs shattering two and entered his heart exploding it killing him. Tye rolled to his right as two bullets kicked up dirt in front of him then fired another shot which missed its target. He rolled again and fired again this time a third warrior was the victim of his Henry. The remaining three stood and broke into a run for their horse. A shot from Jesse took one down and Tye took one of the two remaining Indians. The third made it to the ponies and leapt onto one of the ponies back a nudged the pony into a full out run.

Knowing if he got away he would have a whole damn lot of them back shortly. Tye took careful aim, exhaled and holding his breath squeezed the trigger slowly. The rifle bucked against his shoulder and a instant later the warrior threw his arms up and fell backwards off his racing pony. Luckily the pony slowed and stopped and walked back to where the warrior lay.

Thank God, Tye thought. *That horse returning to the camp would be as bad as the warrior getting there. They would backtrack the pony here.* At that instant he heard another horse running and turning his head saw Jesse already a couple hundred yards away heading due west. Nor wanting to leave any man suffering, Tye ran down the hill to where Sandy stood, jerked the picket line from the ground and after putting it the saddle bag he mounted Sandy and raced him around the hill to check on the warriors. A couple minutes later after seeing they were all dead he headed after Jesse holding Sandy at a steady trot that he could hold for miles. He knew Jesse's horse would tire quickly at the pace he was running now but he figured Jesse, like most outlaws, knew the limits of their horses.

He must have known who ever helped him back there was chasing him. That's the reason he didn't wait around to say thanks. He knows I'm back here so he might just try to lay a little surprise for me. Sam told me he was smart and meaner than a she wolf with pups so from here on it's going to be real interesting.

Chapter Two

I cannot figure out how the army found us, Jesse thought as he squatted behind some cedars on the crest of a small hill watching his back trail for someone following trailing him. *For that matter why in hell was the army chasing us. We didn't rob a payroll or kill any soldiers. How did they find us when the Comanche hadn't?* "Damn!" he cursed. *Here I am in God knows where with no food and one stinking canteen of water. I don't have a clue whether I'm still in Comanche territory or if I am even still in Texas or not.*

He looked up at the sun and set a course due west which he figured was the shortest route to do two things, get out of Comanche territory and out of the state of Texas into the territory called New Mexico. *I don't think the army will follow me there if they are even still after me. I don't know if during the fight anyone even saw me escape so I may be concerned over nothing. The concern I do know I have is food and water.* He stood up convinced no one was close behind him. He mounted his horse and continued west.

Tye had lost some time and was farther behind Jesse than he was before. He had taken the time to try and cover their tracks by brushing them out with a cedar branch. He then circled to the north for a ways, brushed out his tracks again and angled back toward the southwest to find Jesse's tracks again. He knew the Indians would not be fooled long but every little delay he could cause only helped delay the inevitable fight which he knew would probably come.

He had traveled several miles by sundown and sat on the highest hill he had seen watching his back trail to see if he could see any Comanche following. *So far so good,* he thought to himself. He had seen where Jesse had had stopped a couple times to watch for anyone following. He chuckled and mumbled. "Jesse watching for anyone following him and I'm watching for anyone following me." He shook his head. "That's crazy."

A few minutes later he was surprised to see a small flickering light about a mile or so ahead of him. *Somebody is mighty careless with that fire in the open like that where anyone can see it for mor'n a mile.* He rode for a few more minutes and them dismounted and tied Sandy loosely to a cedar. Taking his Henry from the saddle scabbard he proceeded on foot toward the camp. A hundred yards out he froze in his tracks. One more step would have placed his next step on a fair sized rattler who gave him a warning buzz that said 'tread on me partner and you are going to get bit.' He backed up a couple steps and the buzzing stopped. He detoured around the snake no worse for the encounter but a little shaken. He hated damn rattlers and had many a close encounter with them over the years.

He was fifty yards from the camp and could hear men talking but not clear enough to understand what they were saying. He counted eight but there could be a couple sentries. He pondered the situation. *Jesses could be one of them having stumbled into the little group. He would be leery of anyone coming from the direction he had been so it might be to my advantage to come into the camp from the opposite direction. That might throw him off if he is there.* He tried to think what Sam had said when he was describing Jesse. The thought of Sam brought a lump to his throat and moisture to his eyes. He blinked his eyes and thought. *He had a limp from Sam's bullet and I think a scar on his cheek. Other than that he could not remember except he was a fairly good looking gent.* He reversed his direction and started back to where he left Sandy being careful of the dang rattler.

Twenty minutes later he was approaching the camp from the west instead of the east which if Jesse was there maybe he would not be suspicious. He was fifty yards from the camp when he hollered, "Hello the Camp!"

He saw men scrambling to get their guns. "Who's talking?" A large man was asking.

"Saw your fire and hoped to get a little coffee. Hadn't had any in three days," Tye answered.

"Not what I asked," the big man stated. "Who the hell are you?"

"Names Bill Jameson," Tye replied. "Was traveling south when I saw your fire and changed my direction a little hoping you weren't Comanche."

"Come on in then and have a cup," the man said and holstered his pistol. The other men did likewise but not as quick as the big man did.

Tye dismounted and looped Sandy's reins to a cedar limb. Walking into the firelight Tye looked at the men and immediately knew this was a group of hard cases, more than likely there was paper out on every one of them. He walked over to the man who had been talking and stuck out his hand which the man took in a firm shake.

"Big bastard aren't you," he said laughing.

"You're a pretty tall drink yourself," Tye said smiling. The man was a little taller than Tye but not as big through the shoulders and had a little pouch around the belly. He hadn't seen much hard work lately. He had a thick black beard, heavy eyebrows over eyes that appeared to be blue but was hard to tell in the flickering firelight. He wore his Colt low and tied down.

"Names Bill Clinton," he said and that there is Jamie Henry pointing to the man furthest to Tye's right. Next to him is "Tex, then there's Jasper, Larry, Mitch, and the last one is another rider that came in earlier, Jesse. Gett'n to be a little crowed out here," he chuckled.

Tye nodded to each man and tried not to show any reaction to Jesse. This was a tough outfit and any cause of suspicion would be fatal. He took a few steps to where Sandy was and took his coffee cup from his saddle bag and walked to the fire and poured himself some coffee.

"Aren't ya'll a little worried about Comanche's or Kiowa seeing your fire?"

The man named Bill chuckled. "Where did you come from anyhow?"

"Southeast corner of Colorado a little town called Trinidad. Headed down to Fort Davis to see a brother of mine." Tye chuckled, "Tell you the truth I really don't know where the hell I am, in Texas or New Mexico Territory. Ain't seen a living soul for a week till now. My horse I figure is plumb tired of my talking to him. Ain't that right Sandy," Tye said loudly and looking over at Sandy. Sandy nickered and nodded his head. Everyone had a good laugh. Bill put a hand on Tye's shoulder and motioned for him to take a place by the fire.

"To answer your question we are in New Mexico Territory, not Texas. Ain't no Comanche around here, only a few Kiowa and they ain't near the fighter the Comanche or Apache are. They are interested only in stealing horses.

"Haven't fought the Kiowa but I've had a few run ins with the Apache and Comanche," Tye said. My brother told me the Kiowa were pretty fierce fighters but then again that was a few years back."

Bill said nodding his head. "Might have been true then but they are pretty well licked now and most that are not on reservations mostly try and stay out of any fights. Like I said earlier, they are damn good horse thieves though."

The man called Jasper spoke up. "You sure look familiar Bill. You ever been down around Fort Inge?"

"Can't say I have but just where s this Fort Inge?"

"Bout hundred fifty or so miles southeast of Fort Davis."

"The answer is no then. Fort Davis is as far south as I've been."

"You carry that Colt like you know how to use it. Ever shot a man?" The man named Tex asked.

"Only two if you don't count Indians. Why did you ask that?"

Bill spoke up laughing. "Hell, ole Tex there thinks he's the fastest man in the whole damn country."

"Never claimed to be fast," Tye said smiling. "Got enough problems without have a reputation following me around and every snot-nosed wanna-be wanting to try me out."

"Tex stood up a big grin across his ugly pock-marked face. "I think you are piece of shit and scared of your own damn shadow."

"Aint no call for that kind of talk Tex," Bill said. "Sit down and be quiet."

"Shut the hell up Bill. This ain't no concern of your'n." He glared at Tye. "I guess I'm that snot-nosed wanna-be that's going to blow you to hell. Now stand up you damned piece of shit.

Tye looked at Bill who just shook his head and looked away. He liked this stranger and now he was fixing to be dead because Tex was quick, real quick.

Tye stood up and adjusted his holster, and flexed his fingers. "Are you sure about this Tex?"

"Slap leather you bastard."

"Man shouldn't die when the last words out of his mouth is a cuss word." Tye pointed a finger of his left hand at Tex. "After you."

Tex's eyes narrowed and Tye knew he was in the process of beginning his draw and he reached for his Colt. Tex had just cleared leather when something hit him in the chest and knocked him a couple steps backwards. He tried to raise his gun to fire but it was heavy, real heavy and he could not lift it. He blinked a couple times and dropped to his knees. He looked down and saw blood, his blood. "What..." but he could not finish as only a bloody froth came out of his mouth. He dropped his Colt and fell face forward his face hitting the ground hard but he didn't feel it or anything else. He left foot twitched a couple times then he was dead.

Tye replaced the spent shell and holstered his smoking Colt. "Sorry about that Bill but he left me no choice." Tye walked to Sandy.

"Where you going?" Bill Asked.

Tye looked at him and then nodded to Tex lying on the ground. "Figure my welcome is over."

"Tex has been asking for that for a long time. Only reason he didn't try pushing James over there to a contest was because James came in carrying a rifle, no pistol."

Tye looked over where James stood and for the first time saw he was not armed. He scanned the faces of the others and saw no threat in them. He walked back over to the fire.

Bill said. "I will say this and I think the other boys will agree that was the damndest fastest draw we have ever seen." Bill shook his head. "Tex was quick and was always pressing people. I really didn't think you had a chance against him."

Tye squatted down by the fire. "I don't like people to see that he said. Word gets around and pretty soon every town you come to some young kid wants to get a reputation by killing you. I've seen it before and it's not something I want.

For the first time James spoke up. "How in hell did you learn to draw that fast? It looked to me like you anticipated his draw and beat him pretty bad."

"Pretty bad hell," Jasper said. "The barrel of his Colt barely cleared leather when the slug hit him square in the chest."

"Spend a lot of nights on the trail by myself to answer your question James," Tye said. "I practice bout ever night sometimes more than a hundred times. As far as me anticipating his draw an old timer that was a knowing man about such things told me something I have never forgot. Don't look as his gun hand but watch his eyes and face. Something will give you the signal he is going for his gun. It may be a twitch, tightening of the lips, or maybe his eyes squint a little."

"What if you too far apart to see something like that?" The man called Mitch asked.

Tye looked at him and chuckled. "You'd better be damned fast." Everyone laughed.

Bill said. "James, you and Jasper drag Tex's body out of camp. We'll bury him in the morning." He looked At Tye. "Guess you think we are kind of calloused about the killing of Tex but to be truthful everyone pretty much disliked him because he was always strutting around and testing people, pushing people trying to make them mad enough to challenge him just like he did you tonight."

Tye nodded. "He was sort of an unpleasant person." Everyone laughed over that statement.

"You know," Tye added, "That anyone within a mile or so heard that shot and may come to investigate and with this fire the camp won't be hard to find." He was mainly thinking of the Comanche that might be following him or any other Indians that come across the tracks of a single white man or two.

"Told you before that we are not in Comanche territory and the Kiowa or not much trouble these days," Bill answered. "Let's get some sleep." Everyone headed to the bedrolls and proceeded to do just that. Tye walked over to Sandy and took the saddle off after removing his ground cloth and blankets. He spread his ground cloth near Sandy and lay his blankets on it. He lay on top of the blanket after rolling his second one up to use as a pillow thinking *It's not going to be chilly enough tonight to need a blanket.*

He lay there thinking about the situation. *Need to figure out a way to get Jesse away from these men, but how? This is a tough bunch but I don't know if they are wanted men or just some hard cases that are traveling together. I don't think it's the latter because they seem to know each other pretty well and it's obvious that Bill is there leader. I didn't recognize Bill or Jamie's name as being wanted but I don't know any other other's last names. Of course they all could be using names that are not theirs just like I am doing. I'm going to treat this situation as if they are on the wrong side of the law. Better to be on the safe side and be ready for anything especially since the one called Jasper seemed to recognize me from somewhere. He could remember any time.*

He lay there with all these thoughts and then he thought of Sam and a huge lump formed in his throat. *I miss you pard. When I get through with this Jesse character I'm thinking I need to think more of Rebecca and the kids and all the time I am missing watching them grow up. You've told me more than once that same thing so I'm going to listen to you ole pard and go back to scouting or find a nice quite town somewhere as sheriff. You will always be in my thoughts Sam.* With these thoughts bouncing around in his mind he drifted off to restless sleep.

Tye woke suddenly and lay there without moving as was his habit till he figured what woke him. It didn't take but a couple seconds as Sandy was standing still, ears pricked and looking into the darkness. His snorting was what woke him up and he knew Sandy well enough that something was out there. Barely moving he picked up a small rock and tossed it at Jesse hitting him on the hat which was across his face. Jesse come awake and started to rise up but heard Tye's whispered voice to be quiet. He looked at Tye who put his finger to his lips indicating for him to be quiet.

Tye pointed at Sandy who was like a statue, ears pricked and staring into the darkness. Jess understood immediately and nudges Bill who was lying next to him. Jesse pointed at Tye and Bill understood and nudged the man next to him which was Jasper. Within a few seconds every man was awake and had their pistol in their hand except for Jesse who held his Henry.

It was thirty minutes before first light. If it was Indians every man knew they would come from the east at first light where the sun would behind them and have their potential victims looking into the sun making shooting with any accuracy a chancy thing. Tye whispered to James to pass the word to pretend to be sleeping but be the hell ready at first light. It was a long thirty minutes for Tye. It was a hard thing knowing in a few minutes your life on earth could be over. He took a picture from his pocket of himself, Rebecca and their two children that they had made by a man that took and sold pictures that had been in Fort Clark a couple months before. He stared at the picture then kissed it and put it back in his shirt pocket. He thought of Sam lying in the ground. *Dammit Sam you should be here beside me not lying in that stinking grave. Why did you have to get in the way of that bullet that Jesse fired. He thought of again what his pard had said to him more than once; riding with you gives a man a lot of chances to get shot, catch an arrow, get scalped or any other of a dozen ways to die. Sam had always laughed when he said it but now...somehow I realize now that it was the truth.* Then thought, *No, Sam knew the risks of a lawman and he accepted them so you need to quit beating yourself up with guilty thoughts. Sam was a great friend and lawman. He will be remembered forever in my heart and I will make sure headquarters know what a man he was. One other thing Sam. I have found Jesse I swear on my momma's grave he will be paying for shooting you very soon.*

The sun was breaking over the low eastern hill and the silence was shattered by a whole lot of loud screaming coming from the nearby brush and was followed immediately by a hell of a lot of gun shots both from the attackers and the men in the camp.

Chapter Three

Ten or so miles west of the camp where Tye was another group of men were breaking camp. This was the posse of fifteen men led by The Sheriff of Tularosa where Bill and his men had robbed the bank and killed three townspeople including a woman who was in the bank at the time. It was a group of very angry men that Sheriff Henry Dobbs led and he felt like this bunch would stay on the trail till they caught the bastards. Not only did most of the men had money in the bank but the two men killed were friends of theirs. This was two incentives they had the other was the woman killed: she was the madam of the local whore house and was very popular among the single men and a even couple of the married ones in the posse.

Sheriff Dobbs and his men had been trailing the outlaws for two days and Henry Lightfoot, a local breed, was the tracker and he had told the group last night they were had closed the gap to just a few miles. Dobbs, though no tracker, could tell by the tracks the outlaws had slowed down before making camp last night. They were saddled and on the move just before first light.

~

The instant Tye heard the war cries he was rolling off his blanket. Two or more bullets hit the rolled up blanket he had been using for a pillow as he moved. He heard the distinct sound of a bullet hitting flesh followed by a scream. He paid no attention as to who it was that had been hit as he was firing his Colt as fast as he could work the single action gun. He noticed as he was moving and firing that several of the attackers had fallen. *I figured these men were hard cases and could shoot,* he thought as he fired.

He knew immediately by the dress of the Indians they were Comanche and there were a lot of them, maybe thirty or so. They come out of the brush no more than fifty yards away and were now only twenty or so but the attack broke off for some reason and the Comanche were gone as suddenly as they had appeared.

"What the hell," Bill asked no one in particular. "They would have overrun us in a few more seconds."

"Indians are notional," Tye replied. "My pa fought a lot of them in his time and there is one thing about an Indian he always said, you can never figure what he is going to do. My best guess is that one of those warriors lying out there was there war chief and they have retreated to elect another."

"You mean they are coming back?" James asked.

Tye nodded. Just as soon as they elect a chief. We have better get in a little better defensive position while we can and secure the horses before they pay us another visit."

"For someone who says he had only had a little experience with Indians he sure seems to know about them and what we should do, Bill thought. "Any one hit?" he asked.

Larry answered. Jasper's done for and Mitch is hit pretty hard. Has slugs in his leg and shoulder."

"Shit," Bill cursed. "Larry, get the horses over behind those boulders over there. The rest of you find a hole and load your weapons. Every man now had their rifles as well as their pistols loaded and waiting for the attack they figured was coming.

"Get your canteens too," Tye said. "It may be a long day. I've had a little practice at doctoring gunshot wounds Bill. If you want I'll take a look at Mitch."

Bill nodded and Tye hurried over to where Mitch was lying, moaning and cursing. "Aint gonna help none Mitch by moaning and cursing," Tye said. "Let me take a look." Tye took his Bowie and slit Mitch's shirt. He rolled Mitch over on his side resulting in more curses. He saw no exit hole.

"Bullet didn't go clean thru," he said to Bill. "It's gonna have to come out soon before the infection sets in." Bill nodded.

"What about the leg." He asked.

"No problem," Tye answered. "Bullet went clean thru and no bone hit. Going to be sore as hell for awhile but the shoulder is a different story."

"Can you get it out?"

"Probably, but it's gonna hurt like the dickens." You happen to have any more of that whiskey you were drinking last nite?"

Bill nodded. "I'll get it out of my saddle bags." A minute later he gave the bottle to Tye who in turn handed it to Mitch.

"Start drinking," Tye said. "The more the better."

"Something's going on," Jesse hollered.

Tye looked up. "Didn't take them long to get a new leader. They will be coming again real quick so get ready.

He dragged Mitch to a place a that would be out of the way of bullets.

"Let me have a rifle," he said. Tye handed him one and Mitch laid the barrel on a rock to steady his aim since his left arm was useless. "I can still shoot. If them there bastards are gonna lift my hair they sure as hell gonna have to earn the right." He said working the lever to inject a cartridge.

Tye smiled. *Like I thought earlier. This is a bunch of real hard cases.* Whooping and screaming was heard. "Here they come," he hollered. He scrambled to where his had left his rifle. "Hit the horses first to slow them down otherwise they will be all over us.

At a hundred yards the men fired several times each and several horses went down causing others to stumble over them. Comanche riders were thrown head over heels and some scrambling to get out of the way were trampled by other horses. Some that were thrown never moved. The attack slowed but did not stop.

A deadly rain of bullets and arrows filled the air around the men behind the rocks. Bullets cut the air and whined as they ricocheted off the rocks. Arrows made a whistling sound as they went by and broke against the rocks or stuck in some the cedars.

Tye heard a grunt and knew someone was hit but didn't take the time to sneak a look as he kept firing. The Comanche were almost on them when they broke off again and were running like the devil was after them back the way they had come. Tye saw, or rather heard why. He looked over his should and saw a group of fifteen or so men charging and firing on the Comanche. They reined in when they reached where Tye and the men were. To his surprise they held their guns on him and the others. Tye then saw the badges.

Chapter Five

Tye stood up and raised his hands as did Jesse. He looked at the others and saw Larry was sprawled on the ground on his back obviously dead. Bill was sitting on the ground holding his left shoulder with his good hand and Jesse was bleeding from a scratch on top of his shoulder. Mitch was not hit again but was sitting holding his right arm up.

A man dismounted and looked at each man. When he looked at Tye he raised an bushy eyebrow, spit a wad of tobacco and asked. "I know these other galoots except for you and that man standing over there."

"May I get something out of my saddle bag that will explain who I am?" The sheriff nodded.

"Be damn careful son that you only get what you want to show me." Tye nodded and walked slowly to Sandy and reaching for took of the saddle bags. He walked over to the sheriff and handed them to him.

"There's a hidden pocket on the underside of one of them. Look in it if you will."

"Look in the pocket on the flat side."

Sheriff Dobbs did so and pulled out a U.S. Marshals badge. He looked at it and then at Tye.

"I'm deputy U.S. Marshal Tye Watkins sheriff. "

He looked at Tye and smiled. "Heard a lot about you," he said and smiled. "Thought you'd be eight foot tall." Some of the men riding with the sheriff laughed and most dismounted seeing the threat was over. "What the hell you doing way out in with these son-of-a-bitches?"

"Didn't know there were wanted till just now. I was trailing that jasper over there and when I saw he had joined up with these men I took my badge off and rode into their camp under another name."

"You lying bastard, "Jesse screamed and dropped his hand to grab the rifle lying on top of a boulder next to him. A shot from the Colt that had magically materialized in Tye's hand hit the rifle smashing the stock. The men who had been caught off guard looked in amazement at Tye who drew and fired before they had even realized what was happening.

"Damn," one of the men mumbled. "Did you see that?"

"Hell no," another answered, "but I sure as hell heard it.

"Sweet Jesus," Dobbs said. "I saw it but can't believe my eyes." He looked at Tye. "That was the fastest draw I ever saw in my whole damn rotten life," he said taking his hat off and slapping it on his leg to remove some of the dust.

"Well, I would appreciate each of you if you didn't mention it. I don't need my job as marshal to get harder than it is by the word getting out and all the men wanting a reputation to be following me around and pushing me into a fight."

Tye looked at Bill and Mitch. "What did they do?"

"Robbed the bank in Tularosa and killed two of our friends and also a woman that were in the bank. Shot them down for no damn reason."

"That there woman was a friend of mine," one of the men said drawing a little bit of laughter from some of the men.

Dobbs looked at Tye who appeared a little bewildered at why the men chuckled about a woman dying. Dobbs put his hand on Tye's shoulder. "She ran the local whore house."

Tye nodded but still didn't understand why the men acted like that. A life is a life.

"What were you following that galoot for?"

Tye didn't answer at first but walked over to Jesse. He took the knife Jesse had on his belt in the back and pitched it to Dobbs. He then took off his gun belt and Bowie and handed them to one of the men. "Ya'll excuse me for a minute," he said and hit Jesse a vicious blow to the gut doubling Jesse over. He stood back and waited till Jesse was ok.

"That was a cheap shot you bastard," Jesse screamed. Tye walked up to him and dropped his arms to his side.

"Your turn," and stood there waiting for Jesse to hit him. Jesse cut loose with a roundhouse right that Tye ducked under and then slapped Jesse on the right cheek with his right hand. Jesse roared like a bear and charged Tye with his head lowered aiming for Tye's mid section. Tye stepped aside and the kicked Jesse in the butt as he swept by making him hit the dirt on his face. The men with Dobbs were laughing as hard as they could at the scene.

Jesse lay there a moment and then stood up slowly and turned to face Tye. "I'm gonna kill you one day Watkins."

"Well, you dang well better hurry because you are going to hang pretty damn quick." Jesse charged him again and swung another right that Tye blocked with his left forearm and hit Jesse on the point of the chin with a tremendous right fist that lifted the man off the ground and backwards five feet. He hit the ground and did not move."

Tye walked over to the unconscious Jesse Dobbs. "To answer your question Sheriff he killed several men in cold blood including a couple of women but the big mistake he made was in killing my best friend and fellow deputy Sam Jenkins three days ago when we tried to arrest him and his men. He killed the post commander's nephew at Fort Concho during a robbery. He wants him bad, really bad. I'm taking him back there to hang but I got a real true feeling the trip for him ain't going to be a pleasant one at least if I can help make it that way.

Dobbs smiled. "I understand," he said reaching to shake Tye's extended hand. "Good luck. By the way, Tye, none of us will mention the fast draw a few minutes ago. Hell, if we did it would be a lie because it was so damn quick none of us saw it anyway," he added chuckling.

"Thanks sheriff," and he nodded his head to the others. "And thanks for saving this old boys butt from those Comanche." He walked over to Sandy mounted and then took up the reins of Jesse's horse walked Sandy over to where Jesse lay. He dismounted and picking up the unconscious Jesse he laid him across the saddle. He took some rope and tied his hands and feet together and then ran a rope under the horses belly and tied his hands and feet up snug against the horse's sides securing him where he could not fall off.

"That's going to be a little uncomfortable," one of the men said.

Tye smiled at the men and touched his finger to his hat, nodded and headed east leading the horse with Jesse across the saddle who had come around and was cussing loudly.

Three days later he arrived at Fort Concho much to the delight of the soldiers and the Post Commander. Two days later he watched Jesse as he was hung.

"It's done Sam," he said looking up at the sky. "Jesse's dead. I miss you my friend but you will always be with me." He walked off and wept.

Authors' Note

There were many "tough towns" in the Old West. They were not necessarily as Hollywood portrayed towns in the movies but no doubt it was a dangerous time in our history from 1870 to about 1890. The law was spread pretty thin and men for the most part settled their differences with Mr. Colt which as you have heard before made all men equal regardless of size.

One town, Fort Griffin Texas, is number eight on the list of "tough towns" in the old west. Located at the junction of the Clear Fork of The Brazos and Trinity River in northwestern part what is now Shackelford County in the northern part of West Texas. The Fort was established in 1867 with four companies of the Sixth Calvary to help protect the settlers from Comanche and Kiowa raids. In 1870 a very tough town sprang up just outside the fort know as "The Flat "and eventually became a stop-off point for cattle drives headed to Dodge City Kansas.

With the end of the raids after the Red River War the troops were pulled out of the fort leaving the town's population with virtually no law. Many famous characters visited the town occasionally most notable being Wyatt Earp, Doc Holliday, Bat and Jim Masterson among others. Robberies, muggings, and killings were common place.

This particular time is where the following story of this "Tough Town" begins.

Gary McMillan

Tye Watkins

In

A Rough Town

Gary McMillan

Chapter One

Tye sat on Sandy on a small hill looking at the town he had been sent to by his boss to bring some sort of law and order. The town had become a haven for every type of character the west had to offer: buffalo hunters, trappers, cattlemen, store owners, painted ladies, gamblers, thieves, murderers, and the tough cowboys passing through on cattle drives headed to Dodge City. It was what known as a wide open town and a very dangerous place for the common folks trying to make a living. It was thought that an outlaw gang had pretty much taken the town over and it was his job to clean it up. *"Simple assignment,"* Tye thought and shook his head. *If it is half as bad as what I am told it is its going to be a tough assignment,* he mused.

He took off his marshal's badge and put it in one of his saddle bags in a hidden pouch Rebecca had sewn inside one of them. "No sense in letting everyone know who I am till the time comes," he said to Sandy while scratching him between the ears. He nudged Sandy lightly with his heels and started down the trail leading down the hill to the town known as The Flat.

He had been on the trail the better part of a week and Sandy was probably as tired as he was. He found the livery and paid the man for stabling Sandy and making sure he got plenty of grain.

"Where is the best place to get a room and bath," he asked the livery man.

The man spit a stream of tobacco juice on the ground and said. "Hell mister, look around. This here place ain't no big city we have here so there's only one hotel and it ain't much to look at but it's clean. It's over there," he said nodding his head. "Name's Bill Williams and I own this here thriving business," he said laughing and sticking out his hand.

"Tye," Tye replied taking the man's hand not bothering to give his last name even though he figured being this far from Fort Clark and the Border no one would know him. "Thanks" he said and headed to get a room and much needed bath. It was near noon so he figured after bathing he would lay down and take a short nap to rest up some before I start nosing around and try to get acquainted with what's going on here.

It was an hour before sunset when Tye woke up. *Damn, I must have been more tired than I thought sleeping this long*, he thought to himself. He stood up and stretched a little to get the kinks out, put his shirt on and strapped on his gun belt tying it to his leg. He adjusted it some to make sure it was where he wanted it and easily accessible. Looking in the mirror he figured things looked right and after placing his hat on his head walked out of the room and out the open door of the hotel onto the boardwalk to look around.

He sat on a bench and rolled himself a smoke while looking the town over. Surprisingly, there was a a lot of people on the streets. Businesses, what there was anyway, were closed for the day but there was a lot of noise coming from down the street which he figured was from a saloon. He saw a barber shop, a general store, a jail with the windows knocked out or shot out, and the livery across the street from where he sat. He took a couple puffs and walked across the street to look at what was on the side he had been sitting on. Leaning against a post he looked up and down the street.

He was surprised to see another general store, a ladies clothing store, and a doctor's office which he figured was doing well from all the beatings and shootings that had been reported. He had to meet both owners of the general stores to see which one was owned by a man named Logan since he was the man who had notified the marshal's office in 'San Antonio about all the trouble. Tye figured he could trust him since the man was sincere about wanting things cleaned up in the town but that would have to wait till morning when the stores opened up again. He walked down the street and found there was two saloons one on each side of the street.

He walked to the one on this side of the street and looked over the bat-wing doors to see what was going on. There were six or seven tables half of which were occupied and about half dozen men standing at the bar. All the men were wearing a colt on their hip. Things looked quiet enough. He walked across the street to the one where most of the noise seems to be coming from and as before looked over the bat-winged doors. This saloon was much larger than the first and had probably twelve or so tables all of which were occupied by two or more men. There a dozen more at the bar and as the other all had colts on their hips. One man at the bar had two and seemed to be talking the loudest.

"There's always one everywhere I go," he mumbled under his breath. "I know he thinks there is no faster draw than himself and will probably want to test a stranger." He walked through the doors thinking, *have at it kid and let's get it over with.*

As he figured most men looked up at him when he walked in and then went back to talking with their friends or playing poker: not the man with the two guns. He was watching Tye closely when Tye walked up to the bar keeping four men between himself and the youngster. The barkeep brought him a beer and he turned around and leaned back against the bar and studied the men playing poker at the tables. He held the mug in his left hand keeping his right free.

At two of the tables Tye spotted men he knew were probably professional gamblers looking at the 'spiffy' way they were dressed. All the other tables were occupied by working cowboys or trappers and hunters. One table had two men that were not playing but just talking. By their dress Tye figured them to be local merchants and neither appeared to have a sidearm. About that time one of the cowboys at one of the other tables hollered across the room.

"Hey Mr. Logan did you get the new shipment of Colts in?"

The older of the two men he figured the cowboy was addressing spoke up. "Not yet Charlie but they should be here any day. I'll get word to you at the ranch when they do."

"Appreciate that Mr. Logan."

Finding Logan was easy enough, Tye thought and smiled. He saw the man named Logan looking at him and Tye tipped his hat to him. A smile crossed the man's face. *Maybe he thinks he knows who I am.* Tye started over to an empty table that was next to the two men when a voice came from behind him.

"Hey there stranger. Where you going?"

Tye turned and looked at the youngster. "You talking to me?"

"Hell yes. Do you see any other strangers here?"

"Well, since I am a stranger here I wouldn't know if any of these men or even you were a stranger would I?" Several men laughed at the comment but not the youngster.

He stepped away from the bar. "My name is Jesse Lindsey," he said squaring off in front of Tye.

"Is that name supposed to mean something to me or scare me?" Actually his name was familiar as Tye had seen his name on some flyers that come from San Antonio. He had been in several gun fights but all were face to face. He was wanted on suspicion of an armed robbery in Abilene, but only a suspect in the case. "I can tell you one thing 'sonny,' before you square off in front of a man you might ought to know a little about the man you intend to draw on."

"What's your name then?"

"Makes no difference. My name would not mean anything to you but I will tell you this. If your hand twitches close to your Colts you will be dead in the next second. You can believe that or not, the choice is yours but my advice is to turn around and go back to drinking your beer."

The kid looked at Tye studying him. His right hand hung within inches of the butt of the Colt he wore low on his hip and for the first time noticed the man's holster was tied down. This was either a gunfighter or did he just want people to think he was. "You know I can't' do that now."

"I know that," Tye said knowing no man who in the position he was in being in front of his friends was going to back down from a fight. "If you insist on doing this lets give the people in here a chance to get out of the line of fire." Men were scrambling to get from behind Tye and the men at the bar were moving right and left leaving the kid named Jesse standing by himself.

The man named Logan was upset. He knew how fast Jesse was and if this man was a marshal he wasn't going to live long enough to help him and the other honest people out. He started to say something when the kids hand reached for his gun. It was not out of the holster when he stopped. He was looking down the barrel of a forty-five that had magically appeared in the stranger's hand.

"Le... let's ta talk this over mi... mister," he said in a shaky voice. He knew he should have been a dead man but for some reason this man did not fire his Colt but the damn barrel looked as big as a wash tub.

"Unbuckle you belts and let them fall to the floor," Tye said. The kid, hands trembling, did as he was told. "Now kick them over here and then come over here and sit at this table where we can palaver some." The kid named Jesse did as he was told. Tye picked up the belts and laid them on the table. A low murmur started around the room and it was mainly about how fast Tye had drawn his gun. They knew Jesse was fast but hell, he never got his gun all the way out of the holster.

Jesse sat down at the table and Tye sat across from him. "Did you learn anything from what just happened?"

"Yes sir. I did."

"By all rights I could have killed you and no one would question whether it was self defense or not. You would be just another smart-ass youngster that thought he was the fastest man in Texas that was planted in boot hill."

Tye looked at the youngster who probably was not twenty years old and said. "I don't know how old you are but if you want to see another birthday you had better put those guns up except for work because you are way to slow Jesse. Hell, I've seen a dozen men faster than me and I'm sure there are a lot more and I could have shot you before your barrel cleared leather. Just be thankful you met me and not someone else who would not have given it a second thought about killing you."

Jesse nodded. "I understand what you are saying mister and I want you to know I've learned a lesson today."

Tye leaned forward and spoke softly, low enough the kids friends could not hear saying. "You learned a lesson and you are still alive and your friends saw that you did not back down so it's a win win situation for you. Now, my beer has gotten warm," he said reaching in his pocket t and laying a quarter on the table. Go get me a fresh beer and you one too."

Jesse slid the quarter back to Tye. "I'll stand for the beers." He walked toward the bar.

Tye looked over the man named Logan and winked.

"That was a hell of a thing to do mister. Never saw anything like it before and on top of not killing the little smart-ass you taught him a lesson and allowed him to keep his dignity to his friends. Yes sir. I won't be forgetting this day and neither will anyone else in here."

Jesse came back with the beers and Tye handed him his holsters and guns. "You giving them back to me after what I did?"

"You said you learned a lesson or did you lie?"

"No sir I didn't." He took the holsters from Tye. He smiled and said looking at Mr. Logan. "Do you think you might be interest in buying these Mr. Logan.

"Might be Jesse. Come by tomorrow and we will talk about it." Tye smiled.

Jesse walked away but stopped and said loud enough for everyone to hear. "I learned a lesson today and you won't see me goading people again into a gun fight. This man could have killed me and by all rights I should be dead but he didn't. He also told me I was slow compared to a lot of men he knew that was faster than him"...he paused and added, "as fast as he was anyone faster is just plain scary. Hell, I didn't even see his hand move." He shook his head and walked to his friends and they all turned and raised their mugs to Tye.

Tye tipped his to them and settled back in the chair to listen and try to learn a little about what was going on. He didn't want to tip his hand to Logan yet not knowing who the other man was sitting with him. Tomorrow would be soon enough.

Chapter Two

Tye rose early the next morning and found the restaurant was already open and busy. He walked to a table and sat down and saw this cute waitress coming toward him with a steaming cup of coffee. She had seen Tye walk in and saw immediately he was the best looking man she had ever seen. She introduced herself as Betty and took Tye's order and had a little extra sway to her hips as she walked away. Tye just smiled and attacked his coffee appreciating it wasn't in one of the damnable tin cups that burned your lips.

He saw the man named Logan get up from his table carrying his cup of coffee. Walking to Tye's table he asked if he could sit for a moment. Tye nodded and motioned for him to sit.

"Named Logan, Bill Logan," he said reaching his hand and across the table.

Tye took the man's hand and said. "Glad to meet you. Names Tye."

"What brings you to our little city, Tye," he asked even more curious since the man didn't offer his last name. From what he had received back from the marshal's headquarters he fit the description given him and the man's last name was Watkins.

"Just looking it over. Hadn't been this way before and I like seeing new things and places."

The man leaned forward and whispered, "Your last name would not be Watkins and you are a US Marshal is it.?"

Tye hesitated for a long five second before answering. "And if it is?"

"I hope you are the man the good folks here sent for to help clean up this town and make it a decent place for honest folks to live. Since the soldiers were pulled from Fort Griffin it has become a haven for every type of unsavory characters there is. Why a woman cannot even walk down the street without an escort and even then, it is dangerous not only for her but her escort be it her husband or her beau." He leaned back in the chair and sipped his coffee. Putting the cup down he said. "I figure you are after the way you handled Jesse last night. Anyone else would have shot him dead."

Tye studied the man over the rim of his coffee cup. He might have been a merchant but Tye could see strength in the man. He was broad shouldered, had a neatly trimmed moustache, graying hair that was neatly combed, and the grayish colored eyes he had ever seen. His hands showed that he had done a lot of hard work and when he spoke he looked directly into Tye's eyes which to

Tye spoke well for a man. *Never trusted a man that looks down or away when he is speaking to me,* Tye thought.

Tye leaned forward and said in a low tone, "I'm Tye Watkins and I'm the marshal that was sent here to see if things were as your letter said they were and if so, clean it up." He leaned back in his chair as the lady named Betty brought his breakfast.

"Will there be anything else 'handsome'?"

Tye looked up at her and winked. "This is all I need...right now." He was going to play her along because who besides the barber in a town knows more about what is going on and who everyone is except maybe the girls in the saloons and he had no interest in talking to them.

"Thank God you are who I hoped you were."

Tye said. "You said we a minute ago when you said we sent the letter." Tye took a bite a pancake and added. "Who can I trust in this town to keep their mouth shut about who I am till I can figure out what needs to be done?"

Logan said. "Bill Williams the livery owner, Bill Lewis who's the doctor here, George Robinson who owns the other general store and James Henson the owner of the saloon you were in last night." There is a couple ranchers that are honest hard working men. He paused and added, "We think this spot in the road could develop into a decent town if given a chance but with no law…" he looked down at his coffee cup and shook his head. "Not a chance the way it is now."

"Exactly how is it now?" Tye asked while attacking his food again.

"Tough Tye" he answered. "We have no bank and my store and the others I mentioned have been broken into and what money we had taken more than once. We are family men and do not keep the money in our homes because of the danger it would put our families in so most people know we keep it the store for that reason." He sipped his coffee and continued. "Kinda dumb I guess but we are not gunman, we are just normal men trying to make a living out here. I think, but have no proof that a gambler by the name of William James is behind all this robbing and mugging of decent folks. Another rancher, Henry Gray has increased his cattle herd an unusual amount in the last months I think mostly at the expense of the two ranchers Latham and Bradley I mentioned earlier. "

He continued. "We elected a temporary sheriff awhile back and he was shot in the back two days after taking the position. No one wants the job since then."

"You have a telegraph here?"

Logan laughed. "Not hardly. Closest one is in Albany, about forty or so miles from here."

Tye asked. "Albany is not familiar to me. How long has it been around?"

Logan scratched his chin thinking. "Bout three years. Started in late '72 or early '73 I think."

"I think I will take a ride there and send a wire and see if there are any papers on the men you mentioned." He took out a piece of paper and a pencil and wrote the names of the three men Logan mentioned, Madison, Gray and James. He looked at Logan over the rim of his coffee mug. "Would appreciate it if you keep our conversation about who I am between you and me for now." Logan nodded.

Tye slid his chair back and stood up. "See you when I get back." He took some coins out of his pocket to pay for his meal but Logan stopped him.

"Breakfast and coffee is on me." Tye nodded and walked out of the restaurant heading to the livery stable. At the livery he visited with Williams while the man saddled Sandy.

"Well, you didn't stay long," he said while reaching under Sandy's belly to reach the saddle girth and then running it through the metal ring and cinching it tight.

"Going to Albany to send a telegram. I'll be back tomorrow night or early the next day, "Tye answered.

"I was hoping you was the marshal that we asked the office in San Antonio to send here to help straightened things out.

Tye thought for a moment before answering. *He must be okay if Logan trusted him about the telegram.* Tye stood beside Sandy, elbows resting on the saddle seat. "Logan tell you about the letter he sent to the US Marshal's office in San Antonio?"

"How in hell did you kn...." He paused and said. "You are the marshal ain't you.?"

"Tye Watkins," Tye replied, deputy US Marshal, "but I need for you to keep it quiet for awhile while I look into things. I'm going to Albany to send a wire to see if there are any papers out on some of the men that Logan told me about."

Williams stuck out his hand, "Glad to meet you Tye," he said shaking Tye's hand then had a startled look on his face. "Did you say Watkins, Tye Watkins?"

Tye nodded and asked, "Something wrong with that name?"

"You the scout from Fort Clark?"

"Same" Tye answered.

"Well I be hornswaggled," he said slapping his leg. "Tye Watkins...here."

Tye mounted Sandy, started to ride but turned in the saddle. "It would be better if only you and Logan know for now. I hope I can trust you to keep it under your hat."

"Shor'nuff Tye. I won't say a thing. See you when you get back."

Tye nudged Sandy and trotted out of the livery and toward Albany.

Chapter Three

Tye was on his way back from Albany with the telegram from headquarters in San Antonio. William James, the gambler he had seen in town yesterday, had papers out on him for suspicion of a couple of questionable shootings. The attorney, James Madison, had no papers out on him but was known to be pretty much of a shady character and has been involved in some questionable land deals. Nothing on the others except for Gray, the rancher, who was known to be involved in a couple of gunfights. The fights were in front of witnesses and no warrants were put out on him but he is very quick with a gun and high tempered.

He had been gone for about twenty-four hours and had not had any sleep so as soon as he entered the town and took care of Sandy he would head for his motel room. It was about 10 PM when he walked Sandy into the livery. Bill was there and took Sandy's reins.

"He's had a hard 24 hours Bill so give him some extra oats if you would."

"I'll take care of him Tye, don't you fret none," Bill answered. "Did you find out anything?" he asked looking around making sure no one was near.

"Some Bill, but not a lot other than the gambler Williams has some papers out on him and that the lawyer Madison is a shady character but nothing I can hold him for." He took a

drink from his canteen and asked, "What can you tell me about the owner of the Lazy H Ranch, Henry Gray?"

Bill scratched the back of his neck then looked at Tye. "Dunno Tye. I don't like him much. Seems to think of himself as a bad-ass or something. I know Logan and me have discussed how he has grown the number of cattle on his ranch and he has five hands working for him and a couple don't look they have ever done any work at all but sure as hell don't go anywhere without them guns strapped low on their hips."

Tye nodded. "Thanks Bill. Keep all this under your hat for now. I'll start nosing around tomorrow but for now, I'm gonna get me some shuteye."

"Won't say a word Marshal," Bill said as he led Sandy to his stable.

Early next morning Tye sat in the coffee shop just fixing to take his first bite of eggs when he looked up and saw Logan standing by his table. Tye stuck the fork of eggs in his mouth and nodded for the man to sit. Betty had him a cup of coffee in an instant and refilled Tye's cup.

"Anything else I can do for you," she asked Tye in her most seductive voice.

"Not now," Tye replied and Logan almost choked on the coffee he had just sipped and tried to hide his smile.

When Betty walked away he said, "Best be careful Tye, I think she has plans for you."

Tye laughed. "She'll just have to put a halter on them because I'm married to the prettiest lady in Texas and have no plans to get involved with another woman."

Tye continued eating while Betty brought Logan his food. "Didn't hear you order Bill."

Bill Logan laughed. "I've been coming in here for a long time and always get the same thing so Betty just naturally brings me my plate." He took a bite and swallowing asked. "Did you learn anything from San Antonio?"

Tye leaned forward and in a low voice replied. "Not a lot other than the gambler, James, is wanted for questioning on a couple or so shootings and that the attorney Madison has been involved in several shady and suspicious land deals. The rancher, Henry Gray has killed some men in gun fights but so far witnesses have said they were in self defense. Williams over at the livery said he had a couple hands that looked like they were more than able to take care of themselves with their guns and sure wasn't no cowhands."

"That would be Lester Bates and Jim Coots and Williams pegged them right. They haven't caused trouble yet but I think they might if someone questioned them."

"I think I will take a ride out to the Double B Ranch and the Double L today and visit with the owners, Bradley and Latham. I want their take on what is going on. You say both of them are straight shooters and just honest, hard working cowmen."

"Yeah I do. Both men been here awhile and all the trouble has started in the last few months. You know the reputation this town has as a rough and dangerous place to live and that is something a lot of us would like to see change."

"Reminds me a lot of Bracket three or four years ago. Fort Clark is just across the road on the south side on The Old Mail Road and with a mix of bored soldiers, buffalo hunters, trappers, cowboys, and throw in the saloon girls and of course liquor, you had all the ingredients for a lot of trouble."

"How is it now?"

Tye laughed. "Well we still have our troubles but it's mostly the rough men, men on the run from the law that causes problems occasionally. There is a lot of coming and going by a lot of different men passing through on that road. About three or so years ago the townspeople said enough is enough hired a good lawman and two tough deputies to help him. The people of Bracket backed them one hundred per cent and over a period of time it's settled down and became a place where if you were on the run and passing through you did your best to stay out of trouble while you were there."

Tye stood up and said. "Williams at the livery can give me directions. I'll see you here or at the saloon tonight.

A hour and half later Tye was looking at the Double B Ranch headquarters. He was impressed. The buildings were made of rock and built to last. Everything was neat and he could see nothing that needed repair. Bradley came out on the porch and spoke.

"Who are you and what do you want?"

Tye smiled. These ranchers are like most of the homesteaders in that they are suspicious of strangers and take no chances. Tye could see the man speaking was unarmed but he also saw a rifle from a window pointed at him.

"Tye Watkins and I'm wishing to speak to Billy Bradley, owner of this spread."

"You the Watkins from Ft. Clark?" Bradley asked.

"Yes Sir."

Tye saw the man turn and said something and the rifle much to his relief disappeared from the window. The man came out to where Tye sat on Sandy reaching up and offering his hand. Tye took it and then dismounted.

"I take it you are Mr. Bradley?"

The man nodded. "Just call me Bill," he said. "Come inside and we'll talk over a cup of coffee.

Tye was amazed at the interior. The place was neat and spotless and the furniture was all handmade. Two rockers were made of deer horns and a chandelier was also made from the horns. The walls had several mounts on them: a buffalo head, two huge deer heads, and a longhorn head with horns that must have a seven or eight foot span. As he was looking over the room a slim, very attractive woman walked in with two cups of coffee. Billy introduced the lady as his wife. Mary Ann.

Tye had already taken his hat off and shook her hand. All three sat down at the table.

Billy asked. "What in the world are you doing this far from Fort Clark? Are we looking at Indian trouble coming our way?"

Tye laughed. "I'm not scouting anymore but I'm still tracking down men or trying to settle down things in places like The Flat here. I'm a Deputy U.S. Marshal now, not a scout."

"A marshal. Then what you are doing here? Is any of my men in some sort of trouble?"

Tye smiled. "Not that I know of Bill."

"Then what are you do…" He paused and snapped his fingers. "Bill Logan told me he wrote a letter to marshal headquarters in San Antonio asking for help. You are the marshal they sent.

Tye nodded again. "I'm trying to keep that quiet for awhile. Only people that know as of now are you, Logan, and Williams at the livery. What do you think is going on and why?"

Billy took a sip of coffee. "I know that me and Latham over at the Double L are missing some cattle. I know that Gray over at the Lazy H is increasing his herd to fast to be calving naturally. I can't prove that without getting men killed by insisting I check the brands. He has three honest cowhands, good men, but he has two gunmen on the payroll that look like they have been around a lot of trouble and are still above ground so I figure they are pretty salty. The attorney Madison has talked to me and Latham trying to convince us to sell our ranches to some investors supposedly in Ft Worth. Has papers and all already drawn up just waiting for our signature."

"You interested in selling?"

"Hell no Marshal. I've worked too hard and so has Latham to sell at the price he offered. Besides, the papers just didn't look right."

"What do you mean by that?"

"I don't know. Maybe I was just looking for an excuse to get him out of my house. But Latham told me the same thing. He didn't feel good about the way the papers looked."

"I checked up on Madison, James the gambler, and Mr. Gray. If I was you I would not deal with Madison in any shape or form. He has a record of being involved in some shady land deals. I'm dealing with James tonight because he has some papers out on him for killing some men that may have not been in self defense. Gray is a know gunman and is supposedly pretty fast and the men he has killed were reportedly in self defense."

"What do we do?"

"You pretty much verified what I had heard that Latham is a good man so I'm not going to bother going to his ranch right now. I would appreciate it if you could ride over and tell him who I am and why I am here. Most of all keep it to himself, not his men or his wife are to know till this thing breaks wide open. You two just sit still and see how things play out."

"I'll get my horse saddled as soon as you leave and tell him myself. God, he's going to be shocked that it's you that is here." He laughed and shook Tye's hand.

Chapter Four

Tye took his time on the way back to town mulling things over. *I think the best way is to confront the gambler and get him out of the way. Go into Madison's office and show him up for what he is and get him run out of town. Go to the lazy H and check some brands to see if a running iron has been used and if so deal with that. Also need to get some of the trouble makers out of town and let this place start over.* He leaned forward and scratched Sandy on the neck. "Sounds simple enough doesn't it old boy." Sandy nodded his head and Tye laughed.

It was mid afternoon when he rode back into town and stabled Sandy. He walked across the street and entered the saloon. The first person he saw was Logan who motioned Tye to come over to his table which was against the back wall. As soon as Tye sat down Logan leaned forward and whispered.

"The word is out about who you are and why you are here." Tye looked at him and started to ask how but Logan continued. "That man over there standing at the end of the bar knows you and spilled the beans. The whole damn town is wondering why the hell Tye Watkins is here."

"Damn!" Tye looked at the man but did not recognize him. "Who is he?"

"Don't know for sure. He's been asking if any of the ranches are looking for cowhands. Been around here for a week or so."

Tye stood up and walked to the bar where the cowboy stood. He could not help but notice the others watching him and he could hear their muttering to each other. He walked up to the man.

"Do I know you?"

The man stuck out his hand. "No sir, no reason for you to. My name is Jesse Arnold and my uncle Del Arnold, is a sergeant at Ft Clark. I seen you about a year ago when I was there visiting him."

"Damn, you're Sergeant Arnold's nephew. I remember meeting you back then," he said shaking the man's hand. "What are you doing here?"

"Looking for work but there's no jobs at the three ranches here so I'll probably be moseying on down the road in a day or two."

Tye looked him over and was surprised how much he reminded him of his late partner Sam. He had a gun strapped to his leg. "You know how to use that," Tye asked looking down at the Colt.

"I guess I'm a fair hand. I know which end the bullet comes out," he said laughing.

"Well if you are anything like you're uncle you're a man that can be counted on."

Jesse looked at Tye and smiled. "I like to think I am."

"I'm fixing to confront that gambler over there and it might get a little nasty. I don't know any of the people here except the gent I was talking to over at that table so I don't know if any are his friends or not. Would you watch my back?"

"Sure as hell will Tye. Don't you fret about someone shooting you in the back."

Tye nodded and walked to the table where James was involved in a card game with two other men.

"William James," Tye said loudly. The place got suddenly quiet.

The gambler looked up and smiled. "What can I do for you Mr. Watkins, or should I say Marshal."

"Got a telegram here that says you are wanted for questioning about come killings."

James laid his cards down. "You must be mistaken. I have killed no one."

"Then you shouldn't mind answering some questions should you?" The man scooted his chair back and stood up. Tye had only seen him sitting and he was a lot bigger than Tye expected.

"I told you I have killed no one and I sure am not going to waste my time answering questions about something I have not done."

"In the telegram it mentioned a long scar on the man named James's left forearm. Let's take a look and maybe this will all be cleared up." Tye took a step toward the man and instantly the man's right hand flashed down toward the handle of his colt tied down on his right leg.

The next instant would be talked about for a long time by the men who sat watching this drama being played out before them. In that instant Tye drew his pistol and it was cocked and aimed at the man's chest before the barrel of James's gun had cleared leather. The gambler froze realizing in that moment he was looking at sure death.

Tye looked at him and smiled. "What's it going to be James, you going to drop that gun or are you gonna die right here."

Sweat was running down the gamblers face as he chewed his lower lip trying to make up his mind. "I'll drop my gun Marshal."

"Then do it with two fingers and very slowly."

James gun and holster hit the wooden floor. Tye kicked them to the side and stepped toward the killer.

"Turn around and put your hands behind your back," Tye ordered. James did as he was told but as he turned to the left his right fish came at Tye's head. Tye stepped back and said. "So that's what you want? A chance to whip me?"

"Your reputation is way over-blown Marshal. Yeah, I'd love the chance to whip your butt."

Everyone including James saw the smile across the marshal's face as he undone his gun belt and handed it to Arnold. "Hold this for me please." He turned back to James. "I'm all yours so take your best shot."

James immediately let out a growl like a bear and charged Tye. Tye stepped aside at the last instant and tripped the man who hit the floor hard on his face and chest. James stood up and wiped sawdust from his face. The look in the gamblers eyes were pure hate.

Some of the men moved the tables to make room for they figured was going to be a rough and tumble knock'um down fight. They did not know Tye very well.

The outlaw moved to his left then quickly stepped forward with his right foot and let loose a roundhouse right fist aimed at Tye's head. The only problem for James was Tye's head disappeared as he ducked the blow and buried his right fist in the James's belly. James fell to his knees gasping, trying to suck some air back into his body

Tye stood over for a few seconds and then reaching down pulled the man to his feet. "I'll give you one minute to get yourself back together and then I'll continue to allow you to let's see, how did you put it? Oh yeah you said you were going to whip my butt." Every man in the saloon laughed at the remark. A minute later James rolled his shoulders and circled Tye feinting with his left and right as he moved. Tye stood still just turning on the balls of his feet so he would stay facing the man. The man swung a right that Tye blocked with his left forearm and hit James flush on the nose with a huge right. Blood sprayed out of James's nose and those that could see his face knew it would never be as before. It was flatten like a pan cake.

"Come on James, give it up." Tye said hoping the man would.

James swung again this time with his left and caught Tye on the right cheek. Tye moved into the man swinging rights and lefts to the man's face and in the stomach. James swayed a little and Tye caught him under the chin with a right that came from the floor and lifted the man off his feet and onto the top of a table. James lay there with his arms and legs hanging almost to the floor. He was out cold.

Tye walked over to the man and raised the sleeve on the man's left arm. It was there for all to see: a long scar obviously from a knife blade. Tye rolled James off the table to the floor. He took some cuffs from his belt and handcuffed the man. He searched for weapons and found a knife in his boot.

"Arnold," Tye said. "Can you take this piece of trash and deposit him in the jail for me. I want to talk to these good folks."

"Will do, Tye."

Everyone sat down and it was quiet now that the excitement was over and each man wondered what Tye had to say.

"I guess that now the cat's out of the bag and you know who I am ya'll are wondering what I am doing here in your town. There was a rumor in San Antonio at the marshal's headquarter that a problem was developing here as far as killings, cattle rustling and about everything else that is illegal in Texas. I sent a telegram to headquarters about some of your citizens and it seems there are a lot of shady characters here and the gambler, James was one of them. I intend to question the others and see if we can this town a place for decent folks that can walk the streets without fear of being robbed, beat up or worse. So I'm asking you to spread the word who I am and why I am here and maybe some of the cockroaches will come out of the wood work looking for me."

"Damn, Marshal, that's making you a sure fire target to get shot in the back by some of these men who are afraid to face you."

Tye smiled and said. "That's a good point but to tell you the truth I have been on a wanted poster by the Apaches for years and I'm still standing." He started for the door and stopped and turned around. "You don't have any Apaches around here do you?" He asked with a frightened look on his face.

Everyone laughed and one man said, "That look on your face just then, that scared look you just made, is probably going to be on some men's faces when they hear the news." Men laughed again.

Tye nodded. "There's going to be some men who are wondering if they are on that list." He walked out the door and headed for the restaurant unaware of the things being said by the men in the saloon.

Some of the comments centered on the fast draw they had just witnessed, the way he toyed with the gambler in the fight, but mostly on the fact that one of the most famous men at that time in Texas was in their little town. There was a lot of excitement and anxiety about what was going to happen. They didn't have to wait long.

Chapter Five

Tye sat down in the restaurant and the waitress, Betty, was there before he got comfortable in his chair.

"What can I get you Tye, I mean Marshal," she asked in a soft voice. Truth was she was excited now more than before when she just thought he was the most handsome thing she had ever seen. *Wow, she thought, good looking and the most famous Indian fighter in Texas.*

"Steak, potatoes, and a cup of your good coffee please," Tye replied and gave her a wink.

"Is that all," Betty asked leaning down a little more than necessary so that the tops of her breast were exposed a little more than was necessary.

Tye pretended not to notice and nodded. "I'll let you know if I need anything else."

Logan walked in about that time with a slim, nice looking lady and seeing Tye walked over to his table and asked if Tye minded them joining him.

Tye shook his head and stood up removing his hat nodded his to the lady and motioned them to sit down.

"Tye, this pretty little thing is my wife, Betsy"

"Very pleased to meet you," Tye said reaching across the table and taking her hand.

"Tye," Logan said in a low almost whispering voice, "Word's spreading like wildfire about what you said in the saloon awhile ago. Hell, riders are already going out of town to spread the word that you going to clean this place up for decent folks."

Tye took a sip of his coffee as Betty brought Logan and his wife theirs. He held the cup up in front of his face and said. "You know what I appreciate about restaurant coffee more than anything? Neither said a word. "It's not being having to use those damnable tin cups you have on the trail that scorches your lips." This brought a smile to Betsy's face and a chuckle from Logan.

Both thought it was strange that he seemed so unconcerned about the situation. "Tye, do you know what's going to happen here," and then added, "and maybe to you?"

"Mr. Logan I do understand the possible consequences of my remarks but this situation could last a long time if something is not done. The best way to solve a problem is to attack it head on and get it over with, one way or another. It's been my experience that frontier folks, the good folks like your selves, if they truly want things to get better, safer, they will fight for it. I have been in this situation before and when push came to shove the decent folks helped if things got to the point to where I could not handle them myself."

Logan leaned back in his chair and scratched his chin. "Yeah, I can see that happening here. There's some good folks here.

"Not as many as bad ones," Betty replied bringing a chuckle from both Tye and her husband. She looked at Tye. "Are you married Tye?"

"Yes I am." Tye replied. "Married to one of the pettiest girls in Texas. Got me twin kids too, a boy and a girl. They are four years old."

"How does she feel about you being gone all the time chasing outlaws?"

Logan looked at his wife. "What a thing to ask?"

"Tye laughed. "It's okay Logan. My wife understands me more than I understand myself Mrs. Logan. Since I was fourteen when I killed my first Apache in a knife fight to help my dad survive a fight with three of them I have been fighting them. When I was a young boy my best friend was an Apache boy my same age. He visited my home and I made many visits to his home. After becoming a scout for the army I was and guess I still am on the most wanted list. I have no skills Mrs. Logan other than tracking, reading sign, and fighting. We both figured tracking down outlaws would be safer than Apaches." He chuckled. "After a couple years of doing this, I'm not so sure. Our plans are to find a nice town that has a school and a Church that needs an honest man as sheriff and settle down."

"To answer your question Rebecca knows how I feel about the good people settling this dangerous land and that it is my responsibility to help them stay safe as much as I can. You being this far from the Border do not know just how dangerous it is there. A man leaving his wife and home going to the fields to work may not be alive by noon. There's Apaches that hate the settlers, there's the bandits too lazy to work and just takes what other men have worked for, and then there's the occasional raiding party of Comanche's from the north. Your nearest neighbor may be miles away, too far to help when trouble comes."

"I've heard stories about how those savages treat white people," she said.

As usual when this is said to Tye he gets a little rankled. "If I was born an Apache I would be the same." This brought a look of astonishment to Betsy's face. "Let me explain to you as I have a hundred times to soldiers that thinks the Indian as an animal. That land our there, even this land here where you are once belonged to the Indians, at least they figured it was theirs since their fathers, and grandfathers, and great grandfathers roamed this land as free men hunting, fighting other Indians, raising families."

"Then we came and took the land from them not offering to share it. Truth is Betsy, they are more civilized than we are in a lot of ways. There is no such thing as stealing from one another, no adultery, and the big thing is they take care of the elders that cannot still hunt for themselves. Others will share their food and clothing, even shelter. The word 'lie' is not in their vocabulary and will fight you quicker for lying to them than any other reason. Their children are worshipped and loved more than anything else by their parents."

"I...I didn't know that, never looked at it that way," Betsy said, then added, "What about the butchery and things like that?"

Tye finished his cup of coffee jut as the food arrived. Betty poured them all a refill and brushed Tye's shoulder as she walked away.

"Apaches did not scalp their enemies until the Mexicans put a bounty on Apache scalps and it didn't matter if it was man, woman or child. No telling how many Mexicans these scalp hunters killed and sold them as Apache scalps. Anyway, I've killed a lot of them over the years and they have killed a lot of my friends including my pa, but I never hated them because I understood them. There now," he said smiling. "I'm off my pulpit."

"You would make a fine preacher," she said smiling.

"Wouldn't that be something," Tye said. "Indian hunter, man hunter, and gunman in a pulpit preaching peace and love." They all laughed.

At that time two men walked in and Tye, with a quick look, knew they were trouble and Logan verified it when he uttered "damn "!

The two men stopped a few steps away and stood, thumbs hooked in the gun belts, staring at Tye. "Something I can help you with," he asked while slipping the leather thong off his Colt.

"You've made some big talk law dog," the bigger of the two men loudly proclaimed, "and we're here to see if you can back your mouth up. Personally, I think all that talk about you is a bunch of horse shit."

"Obviously you two are some of the men on my list or you wouldn't' be here scared to death and hoping I will turn tail and go hide somewhere because there are two of you. Well, as a man who has faced many a screaming Apache charge isn't going to run and hide from two would be bad man so if you want to settle any problem you have with me lets step outside away from these good folks."

At that time Arnold walked in and saw immediately what was happening. "Need some help Tye?"

Tye laughed, "Not with these two bad men," with heavy emphasis on the 'bad. I would appreciate it thought if you looked to see if one of their friends is out there that's going to back shoot me. "

He stood up and his gun suddenly appeared in his hand which the on lookers never saw his hand move. The two men were startled and took a step back. Tye slid his Cold back in his holster. "If you two are ready let's get this done."

The big man, still trying to figure out how the gun had appeared in Tye's hand spoke. "Now see here Marshal, me and James here were just funning you some. Didn't mean a thing about it."

"You two work for the Lazy H?"

The men looked at each other and the big man nodded his head. "Then drop you belts and let's walk down to the jail."

"Jail!" the big man exclaimed. "Why the jail?"

"So I know where you are while I check to see if there are any papers out on you which I'm sure there is. If not, then you will be free to go."

Immediately sweat broke out the big man's forehead and his lips tightened and his eyes narrowed. Tye knew he was going to draw.

"You piece of shit lawman," he hollered and drew. A hole appeared where the first button was on his shirt and the second bullet was one was an inch lower. The other man froze as Tye swung his gun toward him and the man raised his hands.

Tye asked. "Mr. Logan can you get one of the patrons here to drag the man outside before he messes up the floor."

"Will do Tye," and he hollered at two men he knew to do just that while still amazed at what just happened and how swiftly it happened as did ever other person in the restaurant.

"Sorry about that folks. I apologize for this especially you ladies looking at Betsy Logan.

Betsy spoke up. "I don't know about the others in here but from what I just saw I would say that there are a lot of nervous men around here that are wondering about whether they are on your list or not."

Everyone laughed. Another lady clapping her hands saying, "You never said any truer words in your life Betsy Logan."

Tye walked up to the man standing with his arms up and removed his pistol and knife from his belt. "Let's go to the jail and palaver some," he said giving the man a push.

Arnold stood outside the door and joined Tye on the way to the jail. Was a man on that roof across the street," he said nodding to the general store. I"I pointed my pistol at him and he skedaddled. I ran across the street and down the alley to the back of the store but he was about 75 yards away riding hard. Too far for a pistol shot."

Tye nodded. "Thanks Arnold. Good job. I figured those two had another man for insurance. I would have been shot while facing them so thanks again." They arrived at the jail and put the man in the back cell, as far from the front door as possible. "Arnold, would you mind watching the front door so no one walks in for a few minutes." Arnold looked at him and started to ask why but Tye winked at him and said, "James here and me are going to have a private palaver." Arnold understood and stepped thru the open door, closed it and sat in a chair on the porch beside the door curious as to what Tye was going to do. He was sure of one thing though, he was glad it was James and not him that was going to receive a talking too.

Chapter Six

Tye left his gun belt hanging on a peg on the wall in the office before entering the cell where James was who was nervously watching everything Tye did.

"James, this can be easy and quick or it can be drawn out and rather painful but you are going to give me the information I want. It's up to you." He waited for James to speak up but the man did not say anything. I'm sure your boss Mr. Gray is up to his boot tops in no good. I want to know what he is up to." He sat on the wooden chair he had brought into the cell while James sat on the bed. "I'm waiting James."

"I just worked there Marshal. I sure wasn't high enough on the totem pole to get inside information. We, my friend you killed and me just did what we were told."

Tye slid the Bowie from its sheath in right boot and waved it in front of the man. "You know about me James?"

"What do you mean?"

"That I have lived with the Apache, fought the Apache for most of my life and some say I'm as mean as they are."

"I heard."

"About three years ago I had two Mexicans locked up at Fort Clark. They were part of the Vasquez gang who had robbed an army payroll, lined up the soldiers that were on escort duty and executed them one at a time. One of them would not even give me his name but when I got through with him with this," he waved the big bladed Bowie in front of his face, "I had every damn thing I wanted to know from them included a map showing where their hidden camp was. The fort surgeon worked for two hours fixing up his cuts. Now I'm only going to ask one more time for what I want to know."

"But you are a Marshal now...yo..you can't do anything to me."

Tye stood up quickly and grabbed the man's hand and jerked it down on the seat of the chair. He put the point of the knife against the top of James's hand and pressed just enough to cause a little pain and some blood.

"Okay, okay you crazy Son-of-a-bitch. Wh..What do you want to know." James asked his shaking voice betraying his fear.

"That's better. What is the long range plan that Gray has and how is he tied in with the lawyer Madison and you lie to me we'll take this up where we left off and it won't be pretty."

"I'll tell you all I know but like I said I wasn't privy to everything. Gray has been slowly so as not to be real obvious taking cattle from the other ranchers and changing the brands with a running iron. A man named

Wes is the best I ever did see with that iron in his hands. Don't know as I ever heard the last name though."

"Go on."

"In a year or so after selling some of the cattle he was going to start rough housing some of the smaller land owners and buy them out cheap. That's where the attorney Madison came in. He supposedly knows all the loop holes. Don't know if they are legal or not."

"What do you thing Gray meant my rough housing the land owners?"

"You know; threats, fires, maybe killing live stock etc. That sort of thing."

"How about murder?"

"Maybe...as a last resort. Kill the man of the house and buy cheap from the grieving widow. He's killed before you know."

"I'm going to need you to sign a statement to what you just told me."

"I never learned to read or write Marshal."

"Can you sign your name."

James nodded. "Barely."

"Okay James. I'm going to write what you just told me and you sign it." Tye got up locked the cell door and went into the office. He found some writing paper and a pencil and begin to write but was startled by a gunshot that sounded like in came from behind the jail. He quickly was through the door with his Colt in his hand and saw James lying on the floor blood pouring from a wound in his head. Three quick strides to the window and saw a man on a running horse headed away from town.

"Damn and double damn," he cursed and the front door flew open and Arnold was rushing in gun in hand. "What happened?"

"Got James to tell me what was going on at the Lazy H and when I came back into the office to get pencil and paper so he could sign the statement some bastard shot him from the window in the cell."

"That window is eight or so feet off above the ground."

"He must have been standing on his horse and dropped into the saddle as soon as he fired. I was here in no more than five seconds and he was already forty or fifty yards away riding like hell."

Arnold nodded. "I heard the shot and a horse running." He then asked. "What are you gonna do now Marshal?"

"I'm gonna ride out to the Double H ranch and bring some hell and brim fire to Gray and his so called hard cases that are supposed to be ranch hands."

"I'll ride with you."

Tye stopped and turned around. "This is law business and you're no lawman."

"Swear me in Marshal. You'll need someone to watch your back out there."

Tye knew he could swear in temporary deputies in an emergency. "You know what you are getting into Arnold?"

Arnold smiled. "Sure as hell do." They walked back into the jail and Tye rummaged thru the desk drawers till he found what he was looking for. "Not going the formalities just say I do."

Arnold with a big grin said, "I do." Ty pinned the sheriff badge on Arnolds shirt and slapped him on the shoulder.

"That badge will have to do cowboy," and headed out the door but stopped and looking back over his shoulder, smiled and said, "Thanks."

As they walked out the door Logan, Williams from the livery, and George Robinson the other store owner came rushing to see what the trouble was.

Tye quickly explained the situation and that he and young Arnold were heading out to the Double H to bring the problem to an end.

"You know he has several gun hands out there, Logan said.

I know that Mr. Logan but I know what he has done as far as rustling cattle and what he planned to do with the homesteaders and small ranchers around here."

Logan reached out and took hold of Sandy's bridle. "What plans?'

Tye placed both hands on the pommel of his addle and looked at Logan and the men that had started to assemble around them. "The prisoner James confessed some things to me before he was shot and killed thru the window of the jail by a man standing on his horse and rode off before I could get a shot at him. Gray has been rustling castle from the other ranchers a few at a time and putting his brand on them. Long range plans are to harass, even kill the other ranchers and settlers so they would sell or their grieving widows would sell the land to him cheap."

"The Son-of-a-bitch needs to be hung or shot," a voice from somewhere in the crowd hollered bringing some other comments such as 'damn right," "Kill the bastard," "Never did like or trust him', and other comments.

"If you give us a little time Marshal some of us can ride with you," Logan said.

"Any of you ever killed a man or even shot at a man," Tye asked looking at the crowd. No one said anything. "Stay here. Go out there and you would probably get killed because you would have a second of hesitation when push came to shove and a man cannot do that in that situation. Go home or back to your stores."

Tye reined Sandy around and he and Arnold galloped out of town toward a whole lot of trouble.

Chapter Seven

One hour later Tye and his new deputy were looking down at the ranch from a low hill about a quarter mile away. Tye could see no way to get close without being spotted. *Whoever built that house had Indians in mind because everything has been cleared out for a good killing field in every direction. They even have a tower beside the house that probably had a sentry in it.*

Arnold, though inexperienced in such things, knew there was a problem. "What's the plan?"

"I'm working on it," Tye responded. "Well, my pa always said when you had a problem that there was no good answer for just attack it head on."

Arnold looked at Tye and started to say something but changed his mind and simply nudged his mount with his heels and started forward lifting his gun from the holster and dropping it back in making sure it was free and easy to slide out.

Tye nudged Sandy and side by side they rode into the yard of the ranch. Four men stepped out of the bunkhouse and two men came out of the main house.

Tye speaking a low voice said, "If it comes to guns I'll take the two men in front of the house and you try to slow down the others. From the looks of the four take the one on the right first. He looks like he knows which end of the barrel the bullet comes out. The other three actually look like cow hands so don't go shooting them unless you have to." He glanced up at the tower but saw no one there. "Move away from me a little." Arnold reined his mount a little to the left.

They halted thirty feet from the porch where the two men stood, legs spread a little and the one on the left had his left foot a little farther in front of the other the sure sign he had been in gun fights before. His hand was dangerously close to the butt of his colt. Gray stood with his hands in front, thumbs hooked on his belt.

"We need to talk Gray," Tye said breaking the silence that had suddenly came when the horses stopped.

"If you come to arrest me Marshal, it looks like you are out gunned," he said, a big smirk on his face. "I think you might have made a mistake."

"Don't think so Gray," speaking loud enough for the four men by the bunkhouse to hear.

"Who's going to write these men's paychecks when you are dead because if anyone of them makes a move toward his gun I will kill you first for sure. Don't think they are going to risk getting shot when they ain't getting paid." He waited a couple seconds. "What's it gonna be Gray, palaver and get dead."

Gray wasn't expecting this and he was suddenly not so sure of things. Sweat broke out on his forehead. He had heard of the Marshals ability with that gun. He knew he was fast himself, but he also knew when two fast draws squared off there more than a even chance both would take lead. He hesitated but then things were taken out of his hands. The man beside him dropped his hand to this gun and had a hole in his chest an instant later. Gray scooted sideways and drew his gun but the instant delay it took for him to realize the man had attempted to draw he knew he was a dead man as he saw smoke and fire come out of the marshals gun and something slammed into his right shoulder spinning him around and a second bullet hit him hit him high in the back of the thigh knocking his legs out from under him and he hit the porch. The gun, still held in his right hand was useless as he could not move his right arm no matter how hard he tried.

Arnold had drawn the instant the man had drawn on the porch and his aim was true as the heavy 45 caliber slug tore into the man's throat before he could pull the trigger. He grabbed his throat with both hands after dropping his gun trying to stem the flow of blood. He dropped to his knees blood pouring out between his fingers that still gripped his throat. He kneeled for a full five seconds then fell forward face down in the dirt. Like Tye had said, the other three had their hands above their heads hollering 'Don't shoot, don't shoot'.

Tye had dismounted and hurriedly walked to the porch. He kicked the gun from Gray's hand and knelt down feeling for a pulse in the side of the other man's neck. He was dead. He grabbed Gray by the collar and sat up upright against the wall of the house.

Arnold had also dismounted and disarmed the three remaining men and marched them over to the porch where Tye was. "You never checked to see how I did."

Tye looked up at him. "I figured you were like your uncle and when push came to shove you would do your part. Never thought of it any other way nor did I worry none." He stood up and shook Arnolds hand. "When this situation is taken care of there's something I want to talk to you about."

"What's that?"

"I'll talk to you later about it. Right now we need to get those men tied up so I can take a look at Gray's wounds who was moaning like a baby. Tye knelt in front of the man. Let me take a look at the shoulder Gray and quit your damn moaning and groaning or I'll just leave things the way they are and throw your butt on a horse and take you to town."

The bullet in his shoulder had exited in the back and Tye thought it missed the shoulder bones so he looked at the thigh wound. It had exited also. *At least I don't have to go digging around for the lead in either of them,* Tye thought to himself. He bandaged both wounds the best he could while Arnold found a wagon and horses. They harnessed them to the wagon and placed Gray and the three prisoners in the back. They retrieved two other mounts to place the bodies of the two dead men on and tied them to the wagon also. Arnold tied his mount to the back of the wagon and then hopped in the driver's seat and headed back to town.

An hour and a half later they entered the town and immediately a large crowd gathered around them following them to the jail. Dead men strapped across a horse back always attracted the curious. Tye asked a man to get the doc and bring him to the jail. Logan, Williams, and Robinson were on the porch in front of the jail with big smiles on their faces. They were shaking Tye's hand even before he had wrapped Sandy's reins around the hitching post. The doc came a-running about that time.

Arnold spoke up. "Got a piece of horseshit in the back of the wagon doc who thinks he's hurt. Some of the men standing around the wagon and saw the wounds on Gray laughed loudly.

"And moaning like a woman," one man said laughing.

"What happened," Williams the livery man asked.

After telling him, Logan and Robinson what happened at the ranch Tye want into the back of the jail here Doc was working on Gray.

"He gonna live Doc?"

Doc was putting some stitches in the man's back and from the expression on the ranchers face was being none to gentle about it. "He will live Marshal," he said without looking up. "Going to be sore as hell for awhile though." He put the last stitch in and Gray grimaced again. Doc leaned back in his chair and added. "Unfortunately."

"What do you mean,' unfortunately'?"

Doc stood up scooting the chair out of his way. "Now we have to feed him and those others for two weeks or so while he mends enough to stand trial."

Tye smiled. "They drew down on a federal officer which makes them wards of the State of Texas. I figure on taking them to San Antonio to stand trial if I can count on two or three of you town folks showing up to testify."

Doc put a hand on Tye's shoulder. "You can count on that," he said smiling.

Tye locked the cell door and walked into the office where Logan, Arnold and others were waiting. Tye looked at Arnold, "I don't know about you but I could eat the leather off a saddle right now."

A big smile crossed the young man's face. "Well, now that you mention it I could use some vittles my own self."

Logan spoke up. "We'll all go and it's on me."

Tye stopped and looked at Logan. "If you don't mind I have something I would like to talk to Arnold about. We can all get together later. I still have one piece of unfinished business to attend to."

"What's that," Logan questioned?

"I'm going to run the attorney Maddox out of town."

"Can't you arrest him," Williams asked.

"He hasn't done anything wrong yet. You can't arrest a man for what he might do."

Tye and Arnold walked out of the jail and crossed the street to where the attorney's office was located. When they walked in Maddox was walking out with his briefcase in his hand.

"Going somewhere," Tye questioned?

The fat man stopped and wiped the sweat from his face with his kerchief. "I uh...well yes as a matter of fact I...I am. Have a client in Albany to see."

"I know what you were going to do," Tye said loudly grabbing the man by the neck and reaching down at the same time and taking the Bowie from his boot and sticking under the man's right eye, the tip drawing a little blood. "Don't come back to this town and I'm going to see my boss about putting out flyers all around the State about you and your crooked dealings. I think you may be thru in Texas." He threw the man against the wall. If I ever see you again and you are still working in Texas it will be the sorriest day of your pitiful life."

"Ye...yes Si...sir," the frightened man mumbled.

Tye and Arnold walked out of the office and headed to the restaurant. "You handled that well," he said laughing.

Tye laughed. "Let's get something in our bellies."

When the food came and after some talk about what went down at the ranch, Tye said. "I told you there was something I wanted to talk to you about."

Arnold pushed his plate back and said. "I'm all ears."

"You ever been in trouble with the law?"

Arnold chuckled. "When I was about ten Mr. Hooper at the general store back home caught me stealing a couple pieces of stick candy." He waited a second obviously thinking. "I think that's about it. Why do you ask that?"

"Chasing outlaws is a dangerous job Jesse." Tye smiled. "Dang near as dangerous at tracking down Apaches. It's especially dangerous when you are by yourself."

Jesse tensed some as he now knew what Tye was going to ask him and he had wanted it ever since he met him three days ago.

"I had a partner named Sam Jenkins. We were close friends, always had each other's back. He got himself killed awhile back and it hurt, hurt bad and I swore I would never have another partner. Since then with you around to help I can see that thought was foolish." He pushed his plate back a sipped some coffee. "What I am asking is would you have any desire to be a deputy U.S. marshal and get shot at by bad guys and if you stay with me have a good chance to get shot by bullets, arrows, hit with lances, head bashed in with war clubs and finally... scalped. My old partner said I attracted Apaches like a magnet attracts steel."

Arnold thought for a moment. "Do you have authority to do this?"

"Only in an emergency like we just did. You would need to go with me to headquarters in San Antonio to get sworn in properly."

Arnold was real anxious to blurt out 'hell yes' but didn't want to sound too anxious. *Hells bells*, he thought, *who would not want to ride with the most famous man in*

Texas next to General Sam so he asked, "You and Sam bring in a lot of bad'uns?"

"Yes we did Jesse. Some of the worse there was and there's still a lot out there. Sam told me that being my partner we got all the 'horse shit' jobs."

Sam looked at Tye with a expression of bewilderment. "Horse shit jobs?"

"Yeah. He would tell everyone that because of my tracking ability and being part Apache we would get the worse of the lot to track down."

"Did you get the man that killed Sam?"

"He paid for it Jesse...big time."

"I would be proud to wear that badge Marshal and even prouder to be your partner. Never thought I'd live to be an old man anyway," he chuckled. "By the way, what does it pay?"

Tye slapped him on the shoulder and quipped, "Not much but you get furnished with lots of bullets."

Gary McMillan

Authors Note

I have been asked many times over the years, even by my own children, why I continue to write about the Old West when with my story telling (imagination and BS) I could make money writing the popular fantasy books or vampire books, or more recently, zombie books. I know I could make some money doing that but I write about what I love and that's the Old West and its colorful characters. I make a little money and maybe one someday someone will read one of my stories and think' *I'll make that into a movie*. Till then I will do what I love and anyway, it's like I tell my wife of forty years- the time it takes to write a book keeps me out of bars and away from wild women.

To be a decent story teller you have to know a little about what you write about. Fantasy and zombie books were not around that much when I was young. I grew up in the forties and fifties: Roy Rogers, Hopalong Cassidy, Gabby Hayes, Lash LaRue, Randolph Scott, and of course, John Wayne plus many more western stars were mine and the kids I grew up with heroes. My parents loved the old west and in our home there were three types of reading material, the Bible, True West, and Frontier Times. I have a complete collection of Frontier Times dating back to the very first one published and a great number of the old True West.

So I grew up reading these stories and learning how it was back then. I loved the idea that then your handshake was your word, no contracts or lawyers were necessary in most cases. A man's word was his bond.

The sad part of what I write is that very few young people, forty years and younger, just don't give a damn about the old west. They don't have a clue what went on back then because it simply is a small part of history that our schools don't mention much in their lessons anymore like it was when I was in school. They have no appreciation for what their great great grandparents that settled in this country (Texas) went through to make it here in this wild and dangerous land called Texas.

I hope you will continue to read my books and if you are around when I am having a signing drop by and visit. I get a lot of ideas from my readers in these visits like in the following pages. Anyway, I hope we older generation can keep the Old West alive.

The following pages are an introduction to a new series that many of my readers have suggested to me. The Tye Watkins Series will continue but in between will be books about his father, Ben Watkins, trapper or as the early novelist called them, Mountain Men.

The fur industry (mainly beaver) flourished from the early 1800's and started declining around 1835 with the decline of demand for the beaver fur and was over by 1850. During this short time in history the legend of the mountain man was born.

These men were a special breed of men who wanted adventure and the freedom to do what they wanted to do when they wanted to do it. They wanted no one telling them what to do or how to do it. There were no doctors in the Rockies and no law other than trapper law which was pretty simple-murder another trapper or steal from another trapper the penalty was a quick death.

About 3,000 trappers roamed the mountains during those years. Most only lasted two or three years and gave it up or were killed. The only men who got rich were the fur company's owners who bought the furs from the trappers cheap and sold them for high profits. A normal trapper who came to the yearly rendezvous where they sold their furs and after purchasing powder, lead, flour, sugar, coffee, traps, and other essentials they would need to survive another year were lucky to have much more than a couple hundred dollars left for a year's work. Some did well but most just made a living. It was a living though, living with a great sense of freedom.

Put yourself in their shoes and ask yourself if you could have done what they did. Some lived and trapped alone while some trapped in parties of five to ten men. These were known as free trappers, men who worked for themselves. The others worked for the fur companies and there were no love lost between the free trappers and the company men.

You would live year around in the mountains facing harsh winters of snow, blizzards, and below zero temperatures for months on end. You would have to survive hostile Indians who resented you coming into their land and killing their game. You would have to face the greatest danger of all, the fearsome grizzly or 'grizz' as the tappers called them. A simple broken leg or other injuries could kill you. There were no doctors in the mountains so you had to nurse yourself back to health if you were hurt or sick. To survive one had to have keen senses and knowledge of local herbal remedies besides possessing a passel of guts to go along with being able to handle a gun, tomahawk, and knife.

Many men survived years of this dangerous lifestyle and history would show just how important they were to the advancement of western civilization. They discovered passes though the mountains that thousands of men, women, and children would later use to travel to and settle the land west of the Rockies all the way to the Pacific Ocean.

Men like Jim Bridger, Jim Baker, John Coulter who discovered Coulters Hell now known as Yellowstone Park, Kit Carson and many others survived many years in the "Shinning Mountains" known as the Rockies.

This new series will follow Ben Watkins from St Louis to the mountains. It will cover a time in his life from an eighteen year old greener (tenderfoot) to the time of his death when his son Tye was only nineteen years old. During those years he had novels written about him while in the mountains trapping and later became famous along the Texas/Mexico Border when he rode with the Texas Rangers.

I hope you enjoy the series as much as you have enjoyed The Tye Watkins Series.

Gary McMillan

Vendetta

Ben Watkins

In

Mountain Man

Chapter One

"Wal lookee here Jason. This here youngun must think he's Jim Bridger." The man, Will Hendricks, was making fun of the youngster who was dressed out in new buckskins, new coonskin hat, butcher knife, tomahawk, and carrying a Hawken rifle.

"You know Will," Jason said. "That just about the most fearsome looking man I ever did see," he said laughing and slapping his leg.

The teenager tried to ignore the two and tried to walk by them but the one named Will stuck out his leg and tripped him. The youngster hit the boardwalk hard but was up in an instant.

If you two want trouble you just found it," he said and hit Jason with a right that knocked the man several feet backwards. He handed his rifle to a woman who was standing there. "Hold this for me ma'am. It won't be but a minute. A large crowd of people were watching now and most of them knew the two men to be nothing but trouble makers.

By this time Jason had stepped up and swung a right fist at the young man's head. The teenager blocked the blow with his left forearm and unleashed a vicious upper cut with his right landed flush under Jason's chin. The crack of knuckle hitting bone could be heard several feet away and Jason was unconscious before his back hit the boardwalk.

Will, recovered from the surprise punch thrown by the young man confronted him again but this time he had his knife out. I'm gonna teach you a lesson you son-of-a-bitch and it's gonna be the last one you will ever get.

The teenager stepped back from a slashing right that held the knife sucking in his belly as he did. He pulled his own 10" butcher knife and dropped to a crouch holding the knife low, cutting edge like his father had taught him. Will slashed again and the sound of steel hitting steel could be heard as the teenage parried the others blade.

A little frustrated Will thrust straight at the boy's heart stepping forward as he did so. The youngster stepped back and slashed up from down low and the razor-sharp point of his blade struck Will just below the elbow. Will screamed in pain and dropped his knife grabbing his arm with his left. The teenager ended the fight with a right fist flush on the older man's nose crushing the nose and knocking Will out.

"Somebody get a doctor for these two gentlemen," he said wiping his blade on Will's shirt. A round of laughter followed by backslapping.

"Serves those two right," a man in the crowd said. They have been bullying people for weeks," he added.

Another said, "Well they might better be a little more careful who they bully in the future."

Eighteen year old Ben Watkins had arrived in St Louis yesterday and had been astounded at the number of people living there and that everyone seemed to be in a hurry to get somewhere. He rented a room and intended to stay here three or four days to rest up before he started the long trek to the Rockies which he figured to be a two month journey.

He had left his home a month ago bound and determined to become a trapper like the men he had read about in the dime novels. He had just left the store where he had purchased his new "duds" and replaced his old flintlock rifle with the best rifle in existence, the 54 cal. Hawken. He also bought a brace of pistols, a butcher knife and steel bladed tomahawk. He also had new knee high moccasin boots. He had two hundred fifty five dollars left to buy supplies, traps, and other essential he would need on his journey from the money he had saved over the last four years hiring out to neighbors back home.

He was big, six feet two in his stockings and was built the way other men only dreamed of. On top of all this, he was extremely handsome with deep blue eyes and coal black hair that fell to his broad shoulders. He was taught to trap, read sign, shoot and fight by his father who was a man no one messed with back home. He was on his way back to the hotel when he had been accosted by the two men. Their mistake.

A man dressed in buckskins that were well worn approached young Ben. "Names Jim Thompson and who mite you be?"

Ben took the man's hand noticed it was the hand of a man who was used to using them. "Ben Watkins."

"How old you be boy?"

"Eighteen. Why do you ask?

"You figure on being a trapper," he asked looking at the boy's clothes from top to bottom.

"Yes sir. Fixing to get supplies and a pack horse and head toward the mountains in a day or so."

"I'd like to talk to you if can spare a moment," Jim said nodding toward an empty table.

After sitting down with each a beer in his hand Jim said. "I like the way you handled yourself a minute ago with those two. Where did you learn to fight like that? I mean you are still a youngster but handled yourself like a man who was much older."

Ben laughed. "My pa is quite a man back home. Hard worker, well respected but no one messes with him. He started to teach me to track and read sign at a very early age and then when I was twelve he taught me how to fight with fist, wrestle, and how to handle a rifle."

"He taught you good from what I just saw. Listen, Ben, I have a party of six men and we're headed to the Rockies. Most are greeners," he chuckled when Ben looked at him with a questionable look. He added, "Greeners are men who haven't been there before and have never trapped beaver. "

Ben smiled. "I guess I'm what you called, a greener."

Jim smiled. "Anyway, me and James Wilson are the only ones who have been there and I'd like you to go with us. After we get there if you want to part ways and go it alone that's okay. It's pretty dangerous twist here and yonder. Lots of Indians mainly the damn Sioux, Crow, and after you get there you have the Blackfeet and Utes. It would be safer for you to travel with us than going alone and an extra rifle would help us."

After talking a little longer about the mountains Ben was convinced this man knew his way around and could help him with his supplies, knowledge of horseflesh, and maybe tell him something about trapping beaver. There would be lots of time to talk on the journey to the Rockies. He just did not know how much trouble and danger he would encounter before he even got to the foothills of the Rockies.

Vendetta

www.ingramcontent.com/pod-product-compliance
Lightning Source LLC
Chambersburg PA
CBHW050914250626
47155CB00001B/225